KEEP SWIMMING

Kade Boehme

Keep Swimming
Copyright © July 2014 by Kade Boehme

Editor: Tina Adamski
Cover Artist: L.C. Chase
Back Sleeve thanks to Allison Cassatta
Published in the United States of America

This is a work of fiction. While may include actual historical events or existing locations, the names, characters, places and incidents are either the product of the author's imagination or are used fictitiously, and any resemblance to actual persons, living or dead, business establishments, events, or locales is entirely coincidental.

Warning

This e-book contains sexually explicit scenes and adult language and may be considered offensive to some readers. For adults 18+ ONLY, as defined by the laws of the country in which you made your purchase. Please store your files wisely, where they cannot be accessed by under-aged readers.

What They're Saying About
KADE BOEHME

Gangster Country

"The story sucked me in from the start and I couldn't stop reading. The depth of emotions just captured me. I felt the nail-biting tension. I hung on Kade's every word."

— Sinfully Sexy Book Reviews

"This book will throw you a few curve balls and the twist at the ending floored me. The flow of the writing and the story was steady with all the OMG moments placed perfectly."

— MM Good Book Reviews

A Little Complicated

"Perfect for readers looking for missed chances and fate."

— USA Today Happily Ever After Blog

"This book was a refreshingly funny read with just the right amount of angst to remind you that you are reading a Kade Boehme story."

— The Novel Approach

Where the World Ends

"This is a story of unexpected and somewhat forbidden love. A story of secrets. A story of prejudice and its effects on the unsuspecting. It's a story of forgiveness and standing up for what is right. It's a beautiful, heartwarming story that I'm grateful I had the chance to read."

— Joyfully Jay

Dedication

For B.

Acknowledgments

Jackie. You. I wouldn't have made it, no way no how, without you. I couldn't have begged for a better sister.

Wendy. I don't think I ever have the words to thank you. You've been a constant for so long, I'd be lost without you.

L.C., thanks for the hugs and the random late night FaceTimes and lunches and for just being you.

Tina, thanks for rockin' it out. You're a gem. Princess loves you.

Mel, nobody cheers me on like you. You make me smile and keep me going. Thanks for everything.

Last but not least, The Readers. Dear God, the Readers, Reviewers, Bloggers, fellow authors. You've all made this such an amazing journey. You let me do this job I love, inspire me every day to keep going, and I couldn't ask for better readers—readers who aren't just people who buy my books but who are also my friends. You all mean the fucking world to me.

Prologue

Four Years Ago

No, he did not want to answer the door. No, he did not want to put pants on or be sociable. He did not want to think about anything beyond the Britney song on the radio or the beautiful sonogram picture he'd just put on his refrigerator next to the picture of his mother. But whoever was knocking on his front door continued their insistence that he do just that with their incessant rapping.

He wandered over and slung the door open. *Oh, yay.* Marshall's father. Why now? Why today? "Manny, what are you doing here?"

Manny smacked Cary with his newspaper. "This tone. Take it with someone else. I'm here to see my son, of course."

That smarted. Cary winced. "He's not here." Cary turned and walked back to the sofa, where he'd set up camp. There were two day old tissues, a pizza box, and an Xbox remote with his name on it.

The whole house smelled of dust and emptiness. And unwashed man. He'd get his act together by Monday, he swore it. But this long weekend before the opening of his store was his only chance to enjoy being a slob-- a newly-single, soon-to-be-grown-up slob. Yeah, he knew he was supposed to be a grown up already, but with a business of his own and a child on the way... any delusions he had of still being fancy-free were officially at an end. Come Monday, the first day of the first fiscal year of The Barkery by the Bay, he would officially be a responsible adult.

"Are you not my son?"

Cary's head snapped in Manny's direction. "What?"

"I didn't realize my relationship with you ended because Marshall decided to be a boob."

"A boob?" Cary blinked. "How... 1960s of you." He may have cracked a smile. Not that he'd call it a smile, but... anyways.

"In case you hadn't noticed, I was a child in the '60s. Pardon an old man if his vernacular isn't up to snuff."

Cary snorted and fell onto the couch. "We'll let you slide this once."

"I'll remember to write the local news to report this wonderful reprieve which His Highness has granted." Manny shoved at Cary's legs, forcing him to sit up and move over. "How are you, Cary?" When Manny's palm rested on Cary's knee, he felt the beginnings of the first tears since Marshall had packed his things three days earlier.

He cleared his throat. "Um, no disrespect, but what're you doing here?"

Manny harrumphed. "What am I doing here, he asks?" Another harrumph and some shifting around on the messy couch was a not-so-subtle hint he was not pleased. "I can't check on one of my boys?"

"Well, I'm assuming..."

"What happens when you assume?"

"Huh?"

"Don't say *huh*. You sound uneducated. The correct answer is 'You make an ass of U and Me.'"

Cary blinked. "Okay, seriously. Why are you here?"

"To check on you, of course."

"Shouldn't you be checking on your son?"

Manny's glare silenced Cary. "I am."

Cary felt a scalding tear run down his face. "But he's not here. He..."

"He left. I know."

"Then why are you really here?"

"Stop being so obtuse, Cary. You think you sit in on my triple bypass and I just throw you aside? That's not how this old man works. No matter what Marshall does, you are still my son." When Cary snorted, it was all tears. Manny gathered him in his arms, hugging tight.

"That's right. Get it all out. You got your heart hurt. You gotta let it out."

"Why are you being so nice to me?"

"Because, while I understand—grudgingly so—my son's reasons, that understanding is not enough that I discount what he's done to you."

"It hurts."

"So I've heard." Manny pulled Cary in closer. He had no idea why this man was affording him such kindness. But crying on another person, feeling another human's skin was too much to say no to right now. So he wept.

"You'll get through this, son. It's unfair and I wish I could fix it, change it, but you're a good man. You deserved better than this. I just hope you'll accept that I want to be around and that I'd love to still be Opa."

"Why should you?"

"Why should I what? Be allowed to?"

"No." That had never crossed Cary's mind. "Why should you want to? I don't get it."

Manny got in Cary's face, sitting again and staring

with dull green eyes into Cary's. "Because family doesn't forget each other, son. We just don't. I think of what happened with you and Marshall like a divorce. Things may not have worked out, the situation changed, but you didn't lose me as family. A piece of paper didn't make me your family, nor would another piece of paper have made me cut an ex-wife out of my family. I know I'm rambling, but..."

Cary wasn't too proud to fling himself at the old guy, hugging his neck. "No. I.. I get it. And I appreciate it. I'm just so sorry."

"Hush bubeleh. There's no need. Just get that grandson of mine safely into this world, take care of him..." Manny teared up, placing a palm on Cary's cheek. "And don't forget me, okay? I'd love to be around. If you'll allow me."

"Always."

"And do not forget, even when they're a pain in the ass, children are a gift. No one will love you like them. And you will never love anyone like you love them. It just wasn't my son's dream to have a child. You have been excited about it from the beginning. Don't lose your dream, just adjust to make it look different."

Cary's body went rigid. He couldn't help feeling the need to scream, but he held it in. Marshall had certainly forgotten the dream easily enough. Now... God, now Cary was twenty-four years old and headed toward single parenthood. How did hets do this so often?

"I'm gonna do my damnedest to make that little boy happy." *Little boy.* The final straw that had triggered Marshall's jealousy, his resentment. Cary closed his eyes and took a deep breath. He had a son on the way, one he'd be supporting on his own, as well as a surrogate who had medical needs. While she would still be on Marshall's insurance and Marshall had assisted with earlier financial obligations, Cary would need a second job and he'd have to throw his back into getting The Barkery by the Bay open. "Thanks for coming Manny, but I've got a business to get off the ground." In his head he was already making lists, thinking about Marshall's final piece of business advice, given on his way out the door: *"Hire a manager."*

Manny beamed at him. "That's my boy."

*****

"This is the one." Heath patted the hull of the 46-foot yacht. The boat that he'd been researching, looking at for months. He was so close to the day he could afford to buy it, he could taste it. He'd been dying to get off the rigs since he'd started the job. He couldn't deny being a driller on an oil rig was damn good money, especially as a single man with nothing but his dick and time on his hands, but the work was a bitch and he was ready to move at a slower pace.

"Yessir," the owner, Cary's retired boss and friend, Larry said. "She's in beautiful condition. 950HRS on 8V92s."

"Nice," Heath's best friend Kyle said before disappearing below deck. He reappeared after a few minutes, whistling in appreciation. "Sleeps six down there. Think of the parties we could have on this bitch."

Larry laughed as Kyle bounced up and humped

the rails. That was Kyle. A twelve year old trapped in the body of a twenty-two year old. Heath just shook his head. "As I was saying," Heath continued, turning to Larry, "I'll be using it mostly for fishing charters. I've gotten the licensure, now I'm just rounding up the last of the cash for you."

Larry gestured for Heath to follow him back up to his beach-front home. He was selling the Bertram because he'd recently upgraded to a 55 footer. Basically, he had more money than God. Heath wasn't complaining, because the yacht was priced fairly, and it had some great upgrades.

"I'll take the first half now, and hold it for you, then. Let me get a receipt for you," he spoke over his shoulder as Heath and Kyle followed him into his McMansion. "I'll just run to the office and grab that agreement we drew up."

"Actually, I'm only lacking the last $10k."

Larry smiled. "That's great news. You're a friend. I don't mind knocking that last bit off for you."

Heath held up a hand. "No, man. We settled on one-sixty-seven, that's a good price, and I'll get you the whole nut."

Larry put his hands up as if in surrender. "Okay, calm down boy. I just thought I'd throw you a bone. You've been working your ass off for this since I've known you." Five years they'd known each other, five years of itching to strike out on his own, have a boat of his own and kick back. Living his life on *his* terms for the first time since he made one mistake as a teenager.

"Thanks, Larry. But I want to give you the full amount. I appreciate the thought."

"You always were a stubborn son of a bitch,

Cummings. Good to see your dreams finally coming true."

Heath couldn't agree more. He knew he still needed one more boat, though. Kyle would be running this one for him while he continued to work a few more years on the rigs. Two boats and they'd be able to pull in good money, be a real fleet rather than a couple of drunks with a boat.

"Me, too, man. Me, too."

"Let's get you that receipt." And with that Larry headed off to his office. Within moments he was back with the receipt and the legal sales agreement stating the terms of payment of the final ten grand. Heath signed on the dotted line with a flourish, and shook Larry's hand.

"So what are your plans for the business? Gonna live like this one day?" Larry asked, spreading his arms, presenting his stately home like a game show host.

Heath looked around, snorting. "No, not quite." Larry had been able to retire from his post as an engineer on the rig because he'd been a miserly son of a bitch who'd saved every penny and invested well.

Larry laughed. "Not looking for riches, huh?"

Heath shook his head. "Nope, I just want a dog."

Chapter 1

Present Day

"Uh, oh," a certain pint-sized boy said. Cary snickered when he saw his son's 'help' had been to tip the entire bag of dog food over in the pen. A swarm of Chihuahuas and Yorkies had descended on the unexpected feast. Gus plopped down on his small butt and laughed when a few of the tiny dogs started licking him.

Cary wandered over, lifting the three-year-old off the filthy ground and swiping dirt from the back side of Gus's denim overalls—the ones he'd insisted on having three pair of.

"Dirty," Gus said, observantly. "Always dirty, lil'a boy" he intoned, pointing a finger at Cary, mocking his father's constant complaining over how filthy one child could manage to get in such short periods of time.

"That's right, you pipsqueak." He started tickling the boy, who flailed in his arms as he laughed the gleeful, uninhibited laugh of the young. "Always dirty." He remembered all the people who'd said to him *"Boys are easier than girls, be thankful it's a boy."* He called bull on that one. Girls may be more emotional, but his hands were all dry skin from being in the water constantly required to keep his son presentable.

But this was okay. Today was doggy day, the one day a week when Gus and Cary volunteered at the no-kill shelter his friend and neighbor Celine ran. He always knew he'd come home from their day at the shelter just as squicky looking as his son. They got sweaty in the hot Florida sun, smelly from cleaning dog poop, and filthy in general from playing with the dogs out in the yard.

Cary's own dog had died the year before and he hadn't the heart to adopt a new one yet. Plus, between his volunteer work at the shelter and running a dog bakery on Pensacola Beach, The Barkery by the Bay, he got plenty of doggy time in. He'd opened The Barkery not expecting much, but loving the idea of providing house-made and commercial organic kibble as well as refrigerated foods and baked treats. The locals were definitely bourgeois enough to shop at such a place, but after his partner up and left, taking his veterinary clinic's clientele with him, Cary hadn't held out much hope he'd be able to support himself and a kid on its earnings. He definitely didn't want to think of that time right now. This was their favorite day, his and Gus's. No need reliving things that were so far in the past and no longer significant.

"Daddy, stop! I need go..."

Cary mimicked Gus's somber expression. "You do, do you?" Gus reached over Cary's shoulder, pointing behind them. His son hid behind his lashes and lay his head on Cary's chest, as he often did when they were around strangers. Cary couldn't imagine where his shyness had come from, but those moments were too damn cute to complain about.

When Cary turned, his eyes met those of one of the other regular volunteers who came to the shelter with slightly less frequency than he and Gus did. Cary smiled a greeting, nodding at the man. The very attractive sun-tanned man, who even made Cary hide behind his lashes. He felt his cheeks heat when the guy, Heath, smirked at the Whitmore boys' matching expressions. For if Cary knew one thing, he couldn't have produced a more spitting image of himself than Gus, had he been a clone.

Cary set Gus back on his own feet, patting his butt to get him moving. "Go on, then. Miss Celine is in the feed room. Go find her." He didn't have to tell Gus twice, the toddler looking once more at Heath before scuttling off.

"Still shy, I see," Heath said. He wondered, hearing the teasing tone, if Heath was talking about father or son.

He thought he'd go with the less embarrassing of the two. "I just got him to talk to his pre-school teacher."

Heath's brows shot up. "I know I suck with remembering time and all, but didn't he start pre-school months ago?"

"Precisely."

"Wow, well..." Heath always got awkward when talking kids. He was good with Gus, when Gus would actually stick around, but it was obvious Mr. Big and Sexy was not a kid person. *What a shame.* Because Cary was finally in a place where he believed his friends when they said he was ready to start dating again. His business was semi-successful, making enough profit to keep him and Gus comfortable, though not rich by any means. He was totally over his ex, which had been a growing process all its own, and Gus was old enough he didn't freak out about Cary leaving him with a sitter.

And damn if Heath wasn't right up Cary's alley. The man was technically up everyone's alley, though.

He had sun-bleached blond hair kept neatly cropped, a gold tan and bright green eyes. And he had the most lickable arms Cary had ever seen. Cary knew the man worked on one of the off-shore oil rigs in the Gulf, hence his phenomenal physique. Aside from loving to imagine Heath's body glistening with sweat as he worked hard, manual labor on his rig, Cary enjoyed how easily the man laughed. He was genuinely kind, from what Cary could tell of their times volunteering together. And Heath's love of dogs was a huge plus in Cary's book.

A feminine hand wrapping around Heath's well-formed bicep, the blonde attached to it appearing from behind the wall that was Heath. *Oh, yeah, and he's into girls.* Figures the one guy Cary'd had any real interest in for years was a dog. This girl wasn't the same one Heath had brought with him the previous month.

Cary sighed inwardly. "Oh, good. You brought extra help." Heath's expression was thankful, obviously pleased Cary hadn't thrown in the obvious "Again..." The assistance was always welcome, and even if Cary couldn't keep his eyes off the other man, Heath had an equally mooning female attached to his side.

"I just love dogs," she said. Her eyes only left her companion to give Cary the briefest glance.

"Thanks for inviting me along, Heathy."

Cary smirked at Heath's eye roll and mouthed *Heathy?* Heath simply shrugged and gave his date an indulgent, drop-dead-gorgeous grin. Cary turned, unable to watch the disgusting display. *Because you wouldn't be looking at him like that if he was your date?*

"I finished up the feedings," he said over his shoulder as he started closing the doors that led to the potty area of each kennel. He turned back to the couple. "If you guys want to do the walks, I can do the cleaning in the back."

"Oh, I can do that since you did feedings."

Cary wanted to scoff at the man for being so oblivious to how grossed out his date looked at the prospect of cleaning up the poopy area of the kennels. He nodded his head toward her. "I'm sure your friend would have more fun with the walking."

"Oh, yeah..." Heath said.

"And with the boy entertained in the back, I'll fly through it."

Before they walked out, Heath turned to Cary. "Thanks for thinkin' ahead." And damn if the man didn't give Cary one of those looks that made Cary's heart stutter. He'd often wonder if the guy didn't swing both ways. No way was he just a closet case, seeming to honestly enjoy his female company just fine when they were around. Hell, he'd even run into Heath in a restaurant or two in Gulf Breeze, publicly displaying his enjoyment of said company. But that look... the almost-longing in his eyes gave Cary pause.

"No problem. Someone's gotta look out for the poor girls." No doubt, because Heath seemed clueless where his dates were concerned. Cary would never forget the time Heath had given the last girl he'd brought along their biggest dog to walk. She'd been dragged ten feet through mud before Heath had realized his error. No wonder she hadn't lasted.

Heath patted Cary's shoulder, chuckling before he walked off. Cary watched the man's well-shaped ass bounce in his camo shorts then quickly shook it off. No point drooling over Heath any more. He had poop to scoop.

Chapter 2

"You must go out," Celine said in her lilting French accent. Cary huffed out an exasperated breath. "This attitude. You're young. Savannah and I were planning a night in anyway. Gus will be fine." She sipped her tea, clasping her bony fingers around the cup. She was clearly tired, lines etched in her face, her long black hair pulled into a tight pony-tail. She'd forgone her usual Bohemian skirts for comfier sweats and a t-shirt.

"You worked all day. I was off. It's really..."

"Nothing. It's nothing. He's a good boy. Aren't you Gus?" Gus looked up from his coloring book and smiled sweetly.

"Good boy," he said. Cary couldn't deny it. Precocious was not a word anyone would use to describe his son. He was quiet most of the time. The only complaint Cary ever had was the mess the boy could create. Other than that, he was easily entertained and rarely fussed. He'd even been quiet as a baby. That had been a blessing for Cary when he'd been adjusting to life with a newborn and two jobs. Celine and her teenage daughter, Savannah, had been life savers at the time, always ready with advice and willing to babysit. Savannah being homeschooled had been a life saver in a couple emergency situations since they had been neighbors.

"Doesn't Savannah have something better to do with her night?"

"She's grounded," Celine said, waving off Cary's concern with a flick of the wrist. "Tell your friend you will come."

I wish I could come. Cary so rarely got a chance to date and the couple of guys he'd made it past a night or two with eventually wigged out over the fact he had a kid. Not many gay men his age had that to contend with. Not that twenty-eight was super young, a kid just wasn't often an issue most gay guys encountered.

Cary looked at the text message from his friend, Kent. Kent was another life-saver, his first employee at The Barkery, now the general manager, who held down the fort so Cary could actually have days off. Since it'd been a long day and they were closed on Sundays, Kent had messaged him to see if he was interested in getting a beer. He really wouldn't mind going out with him, unwinding and enjoying a kid free night over a beer and a baseball game.

"You're sure?"

After some tutting and shooing, Celine had shoved Cary out the door insistently. God, did he have great friends. He'd go through the heartbreaking crap with Marshall all over again if it meant ending up with these people in his life. He only hoped he did as much for them as they did him. He could never repay them for all of their help in those first couple years.

After making the quick trip over the Pensacola Bay, he was parking in front of their favorite tavern. It was an old dive sports bar which catered mostly to gay men who didn't enjoy the club scene. Not that Cary minded the occasional club night, but he preferred to relax with his friend and actually be able to enjoy the game being played on the television.

He spotted Kent within moments of walking in. It was a Saturday, so the bar was fairly busy, the noise level high due to drunk Rays fans chanting from a table as two players rounded home on the screen over the bar.

"Lively crowd, tonight, huh?" He asked, taking a seat next to Kent.

Kent looked up, surprised but pleased when Cary had settled on his bar stool. "Yo, Cary!" They did a brief one-armed hug. "Glad you made it. Good game tonight. The Rays are kicking ass."

Cary didn't bother reminding his friend that he was a Red Sox fan. Kent knew, but since he was a huge supporter of their biggest rival, he had to give Cary shit. "How's little bit?"

"Good, good. Hanging out with Celine, tonight. She practically forced me out of the house."

"Oh, because it's such a chore to come kick it with your best bud and have a beer." With that, Kent waved to the bartender, holding up two fingers. Cary groaned, knowing that meant two pitchers rather than two drafts. When the pitchers arrived, Kent poured up two pints and passed one to Cary.

"Have fun with the dogs today?"

"Of course. Gus, too. Anything that entertains him is a good thing."

"No doubt, my man," Kent said then let out a whoop as he jumped to his feet, sloshing his beer in his raised glass. "Take it home! Take it home, baby!" And they did. The whole bar erupted and Cary reveled in the company of all the grownups, the beer buzzing nicely in his system and the game on the TV. Gus was not amenable to being quiet long enough to enjoy a game at home. No matter how easily entertained he was, hours-long sports programs were too much to ask of a three-year old.

"I finally got that recipe sorted out for those carrot treats you wanted to try for the summer special," Kent said after taking his seat again.

"Oh? Awesome." And it really was. They tried to continually add new treats. Each new dog treat had to be teamed with a matching people treat. Pet owners would wander in from walks on the beach and treat themselves as well as their doggy companion.

"Yeah, it was just a little—"

Kent was interrupted by a man who gestured to the seat on his other side. "This seat taken?"

"No, man. Go for it." Kent turned back to Cary. "Anyway, so I was thinking next week would be—"

"Sorry to keep interrupting, guys, but do I know you from somewhere?" This time Kent and Cary both looked at him carefully. His wide, smiling mouth and mischievous eyes definitely seemed slightly familiar but Cary couldn't place where he may have seen the man.

"I don't think so," Kent supplied.

The guy seemed disappointed by the answer. Kent turned to Cary, rolling his eyes. Cary noticed the leer the guy sent Kent's way. *Oh.* Cary picked up his beer to hide his grin before taking another long swig. Poor guy didn't know he was barking up the wrong tree. Sure, Kent was gay and single, but he was not one for hooking up. He had a less active sex life than Cary, and that was saying something, because Cary and his hand had been about as far as his sex life had gone for the last eight or nine months, the stretch before that even longer.

"Shit," the guy said. Cary and Kent frowned at each other then looked back to the guy whose smile had faltered. He glanced up, looking at the seat to the other side of Cary. "Would it be a huge imposition to ask you guys to scoot down one?"

Cary shook his head but Kent bristled. "You know there are tables free over there," he said, pointing at the empty bistro tables in the back. Cary smacked Kent's arm and mouthed *be nice*. Kent had definitely figured out the guy was hitting on him, so he was turning off what little charm he had. Cary didn't know why his friend was so against being propositioned but he didn't feel right asking.

"Not a problem," Cary said, grabbing Kent by the sleeve and pulling until they'd both scooted over one.

The guy scooted down, planting his ass down in the seat next to Kent and earning a huff from him in the process. He reached a hand around Kent and held it out. "Thanks, buddy." Cary took the proffered hand and shook. "My friend struck out with his girl so he said he's on his way out. We don't get to do this often so..."

"It's cool," Cary assured him.

"His girl?" Kent asked. "You know this is a gay bar, right?"

Cary elbowed Kent. The other guy suddenly looked horrified. "Oh, shit? Really?" He stood and looked around. "You mean... these guys... *all* of them?"

Kent sneered. "You might wanna take the party elsewhere before your buddy gets the wrong idea."

"No shit. Thanks for the warning!" The guy sat back down and accepted a fruity looking cocktail. It looked funny in his meaty hand. The guy was a few inches shorter than Cary's six feet but easily had forty pounds of muscle on him, and Cary was no waif. After the guy sipped his cocktail he turned to them again. "Wouldn't have wanted to drink with straight boys."

"You're an ass," Kent said with grudging admiration. Cary just chuckled.

"That's Kyle, actually." He held a hand out which Kent accepted this time. "And usually it's the morning after before I get called names."

"Well, I don't do the night before the morning after so you'll have to settle for name-calling now. And you really are an ass if you set up a straight friend like that."

"Oh, shut up, Kent," Cary said, nudging his friend's shoulder. Kent was in rare form tonight.

Kyle laughed. "No, it's cool. My boy swings whichever way wants to put out. He's a himbo, but he's good people." He took a drink of his cocktail. "He's a bonafide bisexual." He gave a mock shudder on the final word. "I'm surprised he's coming out tonight. Usually I have to drag him kicking and screaming."

"But he's bi?" Kent asked. "Wouldn't that mean he'd be cool coming out to these places?"

Kyle gave a noncommittal shrug, like maybe he'd over shared. He had been awfully forthcoming for a total stranger. "Oh, here he is now." He set his drink down on the bar and rose to shake hands with his friend. "I was just telling my new friends your life story, here."

"Of course you were," the familiar voice washed over Cary. When Kyle sat back down, he met Heath's eyes over their friends' heads. Heath's eyes widened slightly, face flushing with what Cary thought was embarrassment, until he noticed the pleased smirk he'd seen time and time again—the look that had made Cary think the man was interested, even if just a little.

But bisexual? Cary had been on that ride before,

granted it was in college and boys at that age are fickle; be they gay, straight, or bi, so lumping Heath in with that particular ex didn't seem fair.

But hadn't he *just* been with a woman? And he kinda sucked at taking his dates very seriously from what Cary had seen.

"Cary, right?" Heath asked, walking over to him.

Cary nodded. "Hey, Heath."

"You two know each other?" Kent asked, eyeing Heath skeptically.

"Yeah. We've seen each other around," Heath said, winking.

"Oh, the plot thickens." Kyle sounded pleased with himself. "Aren't you glad I dragged you out, now?"

Heath turned back to his friend. "Shut up, Kyle." He moved over to sit on the stool that Kyle had saved for him. They didn't speak much more the rest of the night. Kyle and Kent provided enough entertainment; Kyle antagonizing Kent whenever Kent wasn't talking too loudly over the television and cheers of drunk sports fans.

Cary was hyperaware of Heath, though. Every time he walked to the bathroom it was like he could feel Heath's gaze on him. He even caught Heath looking at him a couple times when he peeked over his beer mug.

When the game and commentaries were over, the two pitchers of beer killed, Cary checked his watch.

"Oh, man. I should get going."

"What? Why?" Kent blinked heavy lids at him. "We just got started."

"I've been here three hours. And you, sir—" he touched a finger to Kent's nose "—are drunk. Want me to call your roommate?"

Kent glanced Kyle's direction out the side of his eyes. "I think that's a good idea."

Thank goodness. "Cool, come with me." He helped Kent off the barstool. When his friend stumbled after a few steps, he felt someone else step in on Kent's other side to help keep his friend on his feet. Expecting Kyle, Cary was surprised to find Heath was the one assisting.

They managed to get Kent to a bench outside. Cary hoped the fresh air helped, because Kent was beginning to look a little green around the gills.

"Where does your boy live?"

"Milton. I'd take him, but I gotta get home to the kid. This isn't unusual, though. His roommate won't mind coming to get him."

"I can give him a ride. I live in Navarre."

"No, I couldn't ask you to do that." *I don't really*

know you. Other than Heath being bisexual and a dog lover who was good with Gus, even if it was awkward, he didn't know Heath from Adam.

"It's not a problem. I'll give you my number and let you know he got home safely."

"Um, I don't know..."

"You'd be doing me a favor. I really need to get out of here and Kyle will try to keep me here all night." Heath held out a hand. "Give me your phone."

Cary eyed the hand warily before handing over his phone. "I'm putting my number in. I'll shoot a text to my phone." Within a moment, Heath's phone dinged to signal he'd received a text. "I'll even make his roommate call you to let you know he arrived safe and sound. My name's Heath Cummings. I own Seaventure Charter Fishing in Pensacola Beach if you feel the need to call the police and ask them to vouch for me." Heath's eyes danced with amusement.

"Or you could call Celine for a reference." True. He and Celine seemed friendly whenever he volunteered, and Celine was pretty rigorous about screening her volunteers after one of them had run off with some of their dogs a few years back. There'd been a whole scandal involving dog fighting.

"Okay. If you're sure. Just don't take advantage.

He'd kill me."

Heath smirked. "His virtue is safe with me." He leaned closer to Cary. "Yours on the other hand..."

Cary flushed, earning a quiet laugh from Heath. Damn but that was one sexy laugh, all deep and rumbling. "I'm, uh, gonna go..." Cary said, pointing toward his car.

"Have a good night, Cary." Cary wasn't sure how, but the man had managed to make such innocuous words sounds like a promise. A very dirty promise.

Chapter 3

Heath rolled over in his bed, grunting at the way his body creaked. His work was hard on the joints. The night of drinking hadn't helped much. When he'd gotten home to find Becca reading on the couch, he'd pulled out more beer and they traded dating war stories, as they often did. She'd given him shit for the sneaky way he'd gotten Cary's number.

Heath hadn't planned on going out with Kyle the night before. After he'd sent Christy and her dreams of babies and beach houses packing, he'd debated it for a while before texting his friend back. Now he was glad he had, though. Seeing Cary had been a huge unexpected plus. He'd wondered about the guy. They had been eye fucking each other for months, even having a few conversations that piqued Heath's interest in the guy even more, but the little boy had always stopped Heath in his tracks. The kid could have been the sign of a girl or guy at home waiting on Cary. Heath figured the latter. Hell, even he'd almost had a baby, so he knew the kid was not a sure indication of sexuality.

He was pleased to discover Cary was not only gay but single as well.

But the boy. Heath was more clueless with kids than he was how to treat a fuck buddy outside the bedroom. He always figured as long as they were satisfied in bed, the rest didn't matter. Not like he was planning on getting married again. Ever. He enjoyed being a bachelor, thank you very much. And God knows he was not father material.

A kid never stopped Heath from fucking someone blind, but he made sure it was clear he was not in the running to be step-daddy. No way, no how. When his ex-wife had miscarried their baby, the reason for their young marriage which subsequently dissolved pretty quickly, he'd gotten in trouble with her and their parents alike by mentioning something along the lines of having dodged a bullet.

Yeah, it made him an ass. And he was sad in his own way over the miscarriage, but neither he nor Becca had been thrilled over the unhappy surprise of becoming parents at eighteen years old. That ten week pregnancy had changed the course of their lives for good, so he couldn't imagine what it'd've been like with a child to raise. His mother had railed against his not having to face the consequences of his actions, and maybe he hadn't had to fully deal with them, but plenty had changed for both him and his ex during their brief marriage. They had both been willing to be responsible for their mistake, but the circumstances were out of their control.

So no, he wasn't keen on getting involved with anyone looking to snag a daddy for their kid, but those hungry hazel eyes of Cary's had him thinking about banging the headboard a few times with the sexy man.

He got out of bed, pulling on a pair of shorts, and wandered out to the living room. After fumbling around with the coffee pot, he sat at the tiny table in the galley. His quarters were small, but they worked for him. He loved living on this boat, his second boat. Kyle captained his first, running the fishing charter service for him while he worked off shore. This boat was eventually going to be used more often. He was counting the days, hoping to have it paid off in the next year or two. He'd be able to quit working on the rig and run his business full-time with Kyle.

He was so close he could taste it. He couldn't wait to be finished. The guys on his rig were assholes. Roughnecking was still a politically conservative work environment. He wouldn't be coming out to the guys he worked alongside any time soon. If he could just make it through the next little while, he'd be all set. God, but it'd be nice to go to a gay bar and not give a shit if one of your locally based coworkers saw you wandering out the door. He wasn't closeted anywhere else but work, and even maintaining the lie in that small part of his life was stressful. He couldn't imagine what it must be like for guys whose whole lives were built on the set of lies and/or omissions required to keep them from getting fucked over.

"What's with the scowl?" Becca asked as she entered the galley. She went over to the coffee pot and poured two mugs, handing one to Heath.

"Nothing."

Becca snorted. "That's convincing." She settled in the other of the two chairs at the tiny dining table. She was a little pink on her shoulders from the sun.

"Been laying out?" It was a silly question, her skin shiny with tanning oil, sporting a bikini top and cut-off shorts. She would sometimes come hang out on the boat on long weekends. They'd been friends before they'd married and that hadn't changed afterwards. They hated being married, hated their situation and hated living together, but as friends they just clicked. They considered themselves the poster children for why friends should never fuck around.

"Nice change of subject," she said, snorting into her coffee cup. "Oh, you left your phone on the coffee table. It's gone off a couple times."

"Thanks," he said. He went to retrieve it and came back to his coffee. He'd missed a couple texts from Kyle, but it was the last text message he saw that grabbed his attention. Cary.

Thanks again for taking Kent home.

He grinned to himself before texting back. *Not a problem. He survive?*

A minute went by before a response. *Yes. He woke me and Gus up for brunch so I'm guessing he lived.*

"Ooh, is that your crush?"

Heath scowled at Becca's gleeful expression.

"Stop being a spoil sport. You were practically giddy talking about this one," she reminded him.

"He's just a hot guy. Nothing special." *Lies.*

"Uh huh. What's wrong with him?"

Nothing. "He has a kid." *And why isn't that bothering you so much with this guy?*

"Oh, heaven forbid. Can't have that, can we?" She shook her head fondly.

"You know..."

"You don't want kids. Don't do serious. Yadda,

yadda." She stood, taking her coffee cup to the sink. "I have the feeling the love bug is gonna bite you one of these days and you'll be so screwed."

"So you've said."

"You should listen. I'm more wise than you give me credit for."

Heath just grunted, finished with the conversation. "How long are you staying?"

"I'm out tomorrow. I have court on Wednesday in Ocala." Becca was a criminal attorney. From what Heath understood she was fairly good at her job. She was certainly doing just fine financially. She'd made partner a couple years back. She still took him up on the offer of his hospitality when she could. His boat was her free vacation spot and she was quick to use it whenever she was able to get away. *Good thing you don't keep anyone around long enough to get jealous.* Yet another reason relationships were not on his to-do list. He didn't have time for jealous partners who'd try to tell him which friends he could have around and when.

"When are you headed back out?" she asked.

"I have one more week."

"Well, maybe you should hang out with the hottie. What's he do?"

"Nosy much?" In truth, he had not one clue.

"You get grumpier every year," she teased, pinching his cheek.

"And you get more annoying. Fuck off." She laughed, grabbing a beer out of the fridge. Not even noon, he noticed. She must have read his mind because she toasted him, her expression daring him to say something before turning up the beer. He looked at her flatly. She burped and left, laughing at his rolled eyes.

He picked up his phone again, re-reading the messages from Cary. He didn't want to *date* the guy. He did want to see him again, though. Preferably just the two of them. Hopefully their next meeting would involve lots of lube. Because that was what one did with a piece of ass as fine as Cary; no doubt.

"Love bug," Heath snorted. "Yeah, right."

Chapter 4

Cary was no idiot. He knew he'd been had with the whole phone number swap. But the butterflies in his stomach didn't mind one bit. He found himself checking a couple times to see if he'd gotten any messages from Heath. They'd spoken once or twice, mostly for Cary to turn down invitations to spend time on Heath's boat.

As nice as the idea of getting into Heath's bed sounded and as sexually frustrated as Cary was, he didn't want to be a notch on the guy's bed post. Did he? He'd certainly gotten the impression, and had it confirmed with his own eyes, that the guy wasn't exactly looking for a steady relationship. Cary also couldn't just dump his son on Celine's doorstep to go get pounded, even if the guy was sex on legs.

That wasn't what he was looking for, though. Heath was definitely another guy who wasn't interested in sticking around. And he'd been left enough times for this lifetime. He'd learned that lesson often enough where men like Heath were concerned.

The bells over the door to the barkery jingled, pulling Cary from his thoughts. He headed out of his office and into the front. When he saw Heath's large frame darkening the doorway, he paused. Heath's gaze seemed to lick him from across the room.

"Hey," he said.

"I'll be damned. You work here?" Heath asked.

"You could say that. What are you doing here?" His tone was a perfect mixture of total asshole and come-hither. He wasn't sure how it was possible, but Heath seemed even more sexy today than any of the other times Cary had crossed paths with him. Maybe because now Cary knew the guy was funny, that he was willing to help a friend, on top of the things he'd known prior to the night he took Kent home. The mint green polo the man was wearing, which set off his tan and made his green eyes seem even brighter, didn't hurt either.

"I came to pick up a donation for Celine. She said to ask for the owner."

Of course, Celine. She'd been delighted when Cary told her about running into Heath at the bar. She'd been the first in line to shove Cary back into the dating world and he was inclined to take her up on this matchmaking effort.

"You're talking to him," he said.

Heath cocked his head. "Really?"

"Yep." Cary wasn't sure what else to say. "I was just about to lock up for the day. If you want to pull around to the back I'll do that and then bring the food out."

Heath took a final look around and nodded. Cary locked the front door behind him and flicked of the overhead lights, heading back into the store rooms. After pulling out the bags of kibble, he pushed open the door to the loading bay, Heath having backed his truck close to the door. Cary lifted a bag and started when he turned, running into the brick wall that was Heath's chest.

"Sorry," he mumbled. Though, he had to admit, he wasn't too sorry. The man's body was firm, strong and unyielding where he'd hit it. He had to struggle not to imagine Heath naked, and was failing miserably. His cock stirred in his pants, making him almost drop the bag of dog food so he could adjust himself to be less obvious.

"You just have all this extra food to give away?"

Thank goodness, a safe subject. That should distract him enough to ease the ache in his groin. "Well, each bag has a sell-by date." He dropped the bag he'd been carrying in the bed of the truck and turned to Heath, who was doing the same. "I try to get them off the shelves and rotate in new product a week before sell-by. Celine goes through two bags a day so I know it'll get used in time, I just put it aside in the back for her."

"That's... really nice of you," Heath said, shining that devastating smile on Cary. He cleared his throat, hoping Heath didn't look down and notice that his cock had actually gotten harder rather than less obvious. *Oh no. No, no, no.* He picked up another bag of food and rather than throwing it over his shoulder, he carried it in front of him. He could have sworn he saw that damned smirk on Heath's face but no way would he acknowledge it.

After slinging the bag in the truck's bed he turned away from Heath who was also depositing a bag. He shuffled back inside, thankful to see the bags were all gone. Before he could breathe a sigh of relief, two strong arms wrapped around him from behind. One hand cupped his erection as Heath rubbed his own erection against Cary's backside. A gentle squeeze of Cary's straining, yearning cock had him moaning, head falling backward to rest on the shoulder behind him.

Heath let out a sexy, breathy chuckle. Heath

suckled on Cary's earlobe, causing goosebumps to rush up and down Cary's body.

"You're so hard for me," Heath rumbled in Cary's ear.

Cary had words, really he did, but they were stolen when talented fingers stroked him through his cargos. Cary felt Heath shift as the man used a leg to kick the back door shut then spun them, Cary's face pressed against the closed door. Every movement was a blur, but within the blink of an eye, Cary's pants were around his ankles and a hard cock was pressed between his cheeks. Calloused fingers wrapped around his cock, stroking deftly as Heath worked himself off in the cleft of Cary's ass.

"Want you so bad," Heath said.

"Want you too," Cary said. He hadn't felt this kind of need in so long. He'd been neglecting his sex life for so long he was almost completely gone to the hormones, the rush of blood to his cock. All he could do was feel. He knew this was probably stupid. He'd just told himself not to be another one of Heath's tricks, but the searing heat of the cock rubbing over his hole, the stroking hand on his erection was enough to melt his brain.

Suddenly it all stopped and he was spun

around. He'd never enjoyed being manhandled so much before. When he was turned, eye to eye with Heath, he felt power course through his veins at the evidence that he had Heath just as turned on.

"So fucking sexy," Heath said, running his hands up underneath Cary's shirt, pinching his nipples. Cary's pelvis flexed, grinding his bare cock against Heath's. They both let out groans and set up a steady pace, rubbing off on each other.

"Not enough," Cary said. His hands had moved involuntarily to the steel globes that were Heath's ass. He felt like a total slut, but he needed this. They'd gone so far already. He *needed*.

Heath moved in, sucking Cary's bottom lip in and nibbling it before kissing him soundly, tongue dipping in Cary's mouth like it was trying to burrow. They were all arms and legs as they wrapped around each other, leaning into the door. One of Heath's hands slid down Cary's back, over his ass then dipped into the crack, teasing his hole.

Cary's head fell back against the door with a thud. "Please," he begged. He didn't give a damn. He'd been lusting after this man for months and obviously it had been mutual. They were two grown men getting off, giving pleasure and taking their own. He could live with that.

"Can I fuck you?"

Cary pulled back and stared, even as a thick finger penetrated him with a pinching burn. He winced but didn't break eye contact. "I don't have..."

Heath smiled mischievously. "You think I'd ask if I didn't?"

"Uh, is it a good idea?"

Heath cocked his head in that sexy, questioning way he had and leaned back, extracting his finger. "If you need some sort of commitment then I'm the wrong guy. I understand. We can just keep doing this if you want."

Cary considered it only for a moment, their pelvises still rocking together causing a delicious tingling in his balls. He shook his head. "No, no I'm good. Get the stuff." And he really was good with this. He never did anything for himself, he didn't have the luxury. He could take a few more minutes, a little more pleasure.

Heath pecked Cary's lips before zipping his pants and bounding out the door. In less than a beat he was back, shoving Cary toward his open office door. When they stepped in, Heath slammed the door and was back on Cary's lips. Cary took a moment to enjoy the smells of male arousal and Heath's sunny, ocean breeze scent. He smelled like the beach and horniness. His mouth tasted of coffee and it was the best damn coffee Cary'd ever had.

Heath unzipped and pulled his cock out, stroking their cocks together in his hand and dropping the lube and box of condoms on the small computer desk. Cary didn't want to think about what it meant that the man travelled with that stuff in his truck, he didn't give a damn right then.

"How do you want me?" Cary asked into the kiss. Heath turned and sat down, bare assed in the office chair. He reached for a condom, never breaking eye contact with Cary as he rolled it on, lubed himself and stroked himself lazily.

"C'mere," he said, licking his lips. Cary moved in close and gasped when Heath sat up, sucking his cock down in one smooth motion. He cupped Cary's balls, sucking with a skill Cary hadn't experienced in too long.

"Gaaaah," Cary groaned. "So good." Heath hummed, making Cary buck his hips. He hadn't noticed Heath fiddling with the lube, but a slicked finger eased into his hole, then a second and he almost shot his load right then.

Heath pulled off Cary's cock, lips rosy red from abuse. "Sit on it." Cary's whole body shook with at those words, cock jerking. He turned his ass to Heath who gave it a couple of squeezes and a smack for good measure before gripping Cary's hips with both hands and easing him down. Cary spread his legs wide, feet on either side of Heath's legs and lowered himself. The blunt cockhead only hit resistance for a second before it slid in. Cary gasped, Heath groaned as they slowly joined.

"So tight," Heath said, voice straining. Cary leaned back against Heath whose arms came around Cary's chest. And like a couple of randy teenagers they started fucking, riding each other fast and furious. Cary must have lost his mind, no way was this like him. He hadn't done anything this crazy since college. He was fucking this man in his office, their skin slapping and echoing where he did business and made a living for him and his son.

But he didn't care. Every thrust, every coming together had his body vibrating, his cock weeping from relief. Then Heath grunted and grabbed hold of Cary's cock. Cary reached down to help and together they stroked quickly and firmly.

"Fuck, fuck, fuck. I'm gonna cum," Heath said,

voice growing in volume with each word.

"Do it. Cum in me." It felt so good to say those words. Cary's balls pulled up. When Heath lightly bit into his shoulder, Cary lost it. "Fuuuuck." Heath must have shared the sentiment because the chair rolled a little under them as he pushed his cock home, deep inside Cary and shot into the condom with loud, guttural whines that only Heath could make sound so damn hot.

They stilled, Heath still buried in Cary, arms wrapped around him tightly, catching their breath. After a moment Heath spoke. "That was sexy, hearing you lose it and cuss like that."

Cary snorted. Yeah, he had definitely cleaned up his mouth once Gus had gotten into the parroting phase. "Oh, crap! Gus." He sat forward and eased himself off the thick cock that had barely softened inside him. "I'm gonna be late."

He pulled his pants up, hindered briefly by a hand massaging his ass. "God, your ass is made for that." Cary couldn't help his pleased grin at the reverence in Heath's voice. He turned, inwardly preening at the blissed out expression he saw on the other man's face. He admired the long, thick cock and heavy balls that had just give him his best orgasm in a long, long time.

"That was great," he admitted. He refused to regret it. He felt wonderful. "But I really gotta go get the little man."

Heath stood, pulling the condom off with a snap. "Yeah, I should get that food to Celine." He pulled his own pants up and zipped them. Cary was stunned when Heath placed a soft kiss on his lips. "That was definitely nice." Heath looked as surprised as Cary at the words, maybe even the kiss.

That was all that was said from that point on other than rushed goodbyes. He'd probably never hear from the man again. He wasn't foolish enough to think it was more than what it was: really awesome sex. He'd forgotten how much good that could do a body.

Forget the slut comments he'd field from Kent, he couldn't stop himself from grinning all the way home. And it'd been a long time since he could say he'd done that for a reason other than a good day at work.

Chapter 5

Heath shoves his foot into his steel toed Baffins. One more hour of sleep wouldn't have killed him. The previous twelve hour shift had been the kind of hell that left you too tired to actually fall asleep. He'd tossed and turned for hours before deciding to beat off to soothe his nerves. Usually that was the magic that sent him right into La-La Land.

Not this time, though. Nooooo. He'd been so annoyed with himself when the image of Cary riding his cock had popped into his head, the feel of Cary's heat enveloping his cock and their skin touching, that he'd ended up over thinking—something no one would ever have accused him of before. Not until fucking Cary Whitmore. And he couldn't figure out why.

Maybe that's the problem? He couldn't help wondering if he'd just turned that fucking awesome sex into something different in his mind because it *had* been so awesome. He'd been running into Cary for so long, assuming the man would be shy and easily tamed in the sack, only to find out instead that he wasn't afraid to give in and ride Heath on an office chair. It almost felt like the sex gods had answered some prayer he hadn't even realized he'd sent up. He had had good sex with a guy he actually didn't mind speaking to outside the closed doors of the ... Office.

"Cummings, get a move on." The engineer, Chester, banged on the door to Heath's bunk room. His Alabama drawl grating this early in the morning. "A gully warsher's comin' down this mornin'. New guys are fuckin' things up left and right." His voice took on a mocking tone, which wasn't surprising since even with ten years experience, Heath wasn't up to snuff in Chester's book. "They need your expertise." Heath didn't even need to see the air quotes to know the old bastard had used them.

"Give me five!" he snapped. He wasn't any more excited about going out in a fucking sea storm than anyone else. In fact, it sounded like hell.

He only had to make it one more twelve then he'd be heading home in the morning. Maybe he'd take one more go at the offering the sex gods had sent his way. Who looked a gift horse in the mouth? And it'd been a while since he'd gone back for seconds. He couldn't resist that ass much longer, with its shapely mounds, and who could forget the trim line of the man's body, and those hauntingly muted hazel eyes?

Really? Waxing poetic about his eyes? It was official, Heath was losing it.

*****

Heath was always happiest when he had just finally made it home. No more bunks, no more cheap ass motel rooms, just the comfort of his own space. He fell back onto his bed. The sheets on his bed were unmade and smelled of his own fabric softener, the air smelled of sand and sea rather than grease and sun-baked, unwashed flesh.

First order of business was a shower, maybe a beer and some serious sleep time, in no certain order. He feared sleep may take over sooner rather than later if he didn't force himself up from his bed. He grunted as he shifted around to dig a change of clothes out of the duffel he'd thrown on the floor.

When his phone vibrated he took a peek at the

screen. *Cary*. Heath still wasn't sure why he'd sent the first text. People usually came to him. And he was particularly annoyed at the smile he couldn't seem to stop from forming—not wanting to study that reaction very closely.

Yeah, I think I can get away.

Heath shot off a quick response—*Don't sound so excited, man*—before heading for that shower. His cock was hard just thinking about what he and Cary would get up to. The urge to jack off was strong, the lust overpowering. He was practically ready to burst like an untouched virgin. He couldn't shake the strong reaction his body had to the man, though.

It's not like Heath hadn't been with other men before. Quite the contrary. He'd been with guys in high school. Then after his divorce his twenty-three year old hormones had been set free and he'd sowed many a wild oat since then, though no more than many of his friends. He just had a bigger "dating pool". He'd had fantastic sex with a couple of people at this point, one or two even had him coming back for months on end—a major rarity when he'd been younger. But Cary.

Cary seemed to possess every physical trait Heath could think of to push his buttons. The man had the roundest ass Heath had ever laid hands on, a face that was the perfect mix of pretty and handsome, and long lean lines made up his gracefully toned physique. Then there was the man himself. He was a little shy but in a way that seemed he was more humble than actually timid. He was funny as hell, and get the man in bed with a hand around his cock and he was a wild cat.

"Fuck," Heath groaned, banging his forehead against the shower wall. He couldn't stop his runaway thoughts. He kept trying to remind himself *he has a kid, you hate kids,* and *you've been married once and almost fucked up one of the best friendships you ever had.* He couldn't even necessarily say Cary was a friend, but Heath didn't balk at the idea of being friends with Cary. But what about Cary? Could he handle that Heath was never going to want to get married, probably wouldn't ever want to be in something that resembled much of a relationship? He could be faithful to one fuck buddy, he didn't require either multiple partners or sex five days a week. He wasn't twenty-five any more. And he wasn't a man whore, but he didn't do *relationships* per se. He was more of a fling kinda guy. *Especially* with men. He couldn't exactly have an open relationship with one, at least not until he was able to quit working on the rigs.

Of course he wouldn't complain about coming home to that tight ass.

"You're fucking losing it," he said to himself, gripping his cock and giving it a few strokes. He needed to get out of the shower or he'd give in and get off before even seeing Cary.

After drying himself and pulling on a pair of sweat shorts, he checked his phone again. He would be a dog today, though. He was almost uncomfortably horny and had been for weeks. He'd turned down a couple of roughneck groupies when they'd tried to pick up him and some of the guys when they'd gotten back ashore and hit a bar in Texas the night before. He'd had Cary on the brain but he wouldn't be offended if the guy'd intended it to just be a one-off. He could always hit up someone else. It was a Saturday night after all.

Sorry. Had to check with sitter.

Um. That was a bit of a mood killer. *Not a problem.*

I can come for a bit. If that's still cool.

Bingo. He shot off his address and got a response that Cary'd be around in an hour. That'd do. He went for a beer from the fridge and was glad to see either Kyle or Becca had obviously been by and restocked—they helped drink more of it than he did after all. He putzed around checking little things on the yacht, had another beer or two and set out condoms and lube.

Almost an hour to the minute, he heard the distinct thump of feet on the dock and opened the door to the deck. There, looking good enough to eat in jeans and a t-shirt, stood Cary, seeming slightly unsure of himself. When their eyes met, Cary flushed but Heath knew that flush, one of arousal.

"Come aboard, sexy," said Heath. Cary gave him a sinfully adorable look from under his lashes before making his way onto the deck of the yacht.

"You live in a boat?"

Heath scoffed playfully. "A boat, he says. This, my good man, is a yacht. Say that shit to Thurston Howell the third."

Cary raised an eyebrow. "Who?"

"Oh, come on. Gilligan's Island? I'm not that much older than you, man."

"How old *are* you?" Cary asked, eyeing Heath's shirtless torso with undeniable hunger, making Heath's cock start its rise to say hello. Damn, he was so turned on that just staring at the guy's sweet lips made him ready to fuck the aluminum railing.

"Thirty-two."

"Oh, no. I'm twenty-eight." Cary's gawping at Heath's tented shorts made Heath smirk, trying to put on his most rakish expression as he dragged his eyes up and down Cary. A significant bulge had grown in the crotch of his jeans as well.

"Are we gonna keep talking out here and keep the sitter waiting or do I get to ask you inside now?"

Cary looked startled for a moment, realizing Heath'd noticed his staring. Heath moved into Cary's space, going for the same move he'd used to get the man to loosen up as last time. He grabbed a handful of thick cock through the cotton of the man's pants.

Cary let out a shuddering breath. "Sitter's my neighbor. She'll be there four more hours."

Heath stroked Cary's cock and the man shuddered again, breath hitching. Good to see Heath could lead Cary around by his dick as Cary seemed able to do to him.

"Glad you could make it," he said, breathing in Cary's ear.

"Me too," Cary said, though the admission seemed to embarrass him. Heath wondered why, but he was officially over the introductory part of this evening. He pulled Cary into the cabin's open door and shut it behind them. Cary let out an oomph as Heath shoved him against the closed door.

"We seem to be in this position a lot lately."

"Yeah," Cary said on a breath. Heath did something that was equally as rare for him as obsessing over someone, he kissed Cary. He wasn't sure why this activity was one that he'd had in mind almost as much as the fucking, but damn those lips.

When their lips touched, both of them grunted. The kiss was fervent, fast and passionate. Fuck he'd never been kissed like that. Wet and hard and sweet all at the same time. He was loathe to admit, but it made him a little weak in the knees.

Fuck that. He pulled out of the kiss as gave a small growl, noticing Cary's lips seemed to be chasing his as they parted. He went for the fly of Cary's jeans and was pleased to find they were button-fly. With one deft motion, the fly was open and Cary's cock sprung up and out of its cotton prison, arching upward from the trimmed thatch of hair at the base.

"Oh, commando?" He asked, reaching a hand into the jeans to help Cary's balls come into view, rolling them in his hands, loving the sounds Cary made as Heath fondled and stroked. Cary's head leaned back against the door behind him, and again this all looked so familiar. He'd always remember the image of Cary exactly like this, and he didn't think he would ever mind that. He leaned in and licked up Cary's throat before lightly sinking his teeth in the soft skin behind his ear.

"Oh, wow," Cary breathed, hips thrusting forward. Heath dropped to his knees then, taking Cary's cock into his mouth. Damn, but he'd never wanted to taste someone so badly in his life. The urge was overwhelming. As he took the tasty treat all the way to the base, working it with his throat, he pulled his own cock out and started stroking.

"Heath, so..." Then Cary groaned and thrust into Heath's mouth. Heath moaned at the sound of his name on Cary's lips. He started sucking in earnest while Cary pummeled his face, balls swinging with every thrust. The feel of the heavy cock on his tongue, the salty taste of it, the way the balls occasionally hit his chin were working together to bring Heath so close. He was afraid he wasn't going to last if he kept stroking himself.

But did he care? He'd wanted a taste.

"Oh, Heath... I'm gonna..." And that made up Heath's mind. He stroked himself faster with one hand, cupping Cary's sac with the other, rolling the balls quickly the way he liked done to his. Cary let out a gasp and shortly after started spurting down Heath's throat. Heath took it as it came, sucking steadily until he had to pull off and place his head against Cary's stomach for support. His cock erupted in spurt after spurt, dribbling over his hands and onto Cary's jeans.

When the fuzz cleared from his mind, he felt Cary stroking his hair softly. He looked up to see Cary's expression. They stared at each other for a moment, a moment where Heath got lost in those hazel eyes. Those sincere and reverent eyes.

What are you doing?

He leaned back and looked down, grimacing. "Sorry. Got that all over your jeans."

"You came?"

Heath looked up, smirking. "What can I say?" He rose to standing, tucking himself away. "You just tasted that good."

Cary's face went flat. "Are these lines you use on everyone?"

Cary must've been able to see the *yes* written all over Heath's face because he seemed suddenly annoyed and tucked himself away, stepping around Heath. "I need the bathroom."

Heath was confused. Because while yes he did use those lines on other people, he'd really meant it with Cary. He also didn't know why it bothered him so much that he'd seemed to have hurt Cary.

"Sorry," Cary said behind him, making him turn. "I'm sorry I was a dick. I guess... It's just been a long time since I've done... this..."

"This?"

"Messed around with somebody. I forgot it's about using lines and just getting off."

Heath suddenly felt like a heel. "Hey, I'm sorry too. I try not to be a big man whore with go to 'moves'. I just also don't get *involved*. Y'know"

"I do. I knew what this was. I promise I wasn't expecting a ring when I came over. I just... was monogamous for a long time. I've been out of the game since... well, since college."

What the hell? "That... uh, sounds like..." *Baggage.* "Sounds sucky."

Cary snorted. "It has good points and bad ones."

"Hey, look..." Heath stopped the words because he could see Cary was gearing up for a brush off, a rejection. Heath'd never had problems brushing off someone before, but that look... Cary was a decent guy. And he said he knew the score. So maybe it wouldn't hurt to be nice, maybe be friendly. *Not like you haven't fucked the other people you call good friends.* And he wasn't quite ready to give up this piece of ass yet.

"Want a beer?" Heath laughed at the surprise the bloomed on Cary's face.

"Sure?"

"You still have a couple hours before you have to get back to the munchkin. You said something last time about not getting much grown up time. We'll grab a beer, sit on the deck, shoot the shit. It'll be nice to talk to someone other than the old roughnecks I've been around the last couple weeks."

Cary still looked skeptical.

"Seriously. I'm not saying 'let's be friends with benefits', just 'let's be friends.'"

Cary seemed to think on that a moment, then nodded slowly. "Okay. Who doesn't need more friends, huh?"

"Exactly. Though, I won't complain if you want to hit me up for some more of those benefits. That's a fine ass you've got, *friend*." Heath winked, earning an eye roll and a blush from Cary.

Heath fetched a few beers and stuck them in a bucket they could take up top with them. When Cary followed him up they took a seat and looked out over the Gulf, sun having just dipped down out of the sky, leaving a pink burst in its wake.

"This is why I love living here," Cary said. "The views are always gorgeous."

"You from here?" Heath asked.

"No. Originally from New York City. Moved down with my ex about six years ago."

"Ex... like mother of your child?" Heath had always been curious about that situation. Didn't seem like a question that would be out of bounds for a friend to ask.

Cary scrunched his nose. "Uh, no. I'm a gold star. Gay as it gets." When he saw the questioning look he was getting from Heath he laughed. "Oh, you mean Gus. His biological mother is a surrogate from Ocala who needed tuition for her kid's college and had good genes. The ex, Marshall... let's not go there."

"Understood. My ex and I are still on pretty good terms. She's an attorney in Tallahassee, which would be where I'm originally from."

"That's nice." Cary's frown spoke volumes. And Heath didn't know why he was so concerned with what that frown meant.

Well, that was a lie. If circumstances were different, if he did relationships, Cary would be someone he'd go for it with. Minus the kid, of course. He worked hard, volunteered to feed dogs, and had that ass. So far Heath was hard pressed to find many qualities he didn't find endearing, which was about a kick in the nuts.

"This *yacht* is great," Cary said.

"Thanks," Heath preened. He loved his boat so yeah, another point in the Cary column. Dammit. "She's my pride and joy. The *Keep Swimming*."

"Interesting name."

"Well, that's what my philosophy is in life. Life's gonna give you shit. So you can either let it drown you, or you can keep swimming."

Cary was studying Heath close enough to make him want to squirm. His expression was unreadable before he looked back out over the water. "Gus would love this. He's always talking about boats this and boats that. He's been on his grandpa's boat, but he lives down in Miami so I don't get to take him often."

"Well, why don't you bring him out one day?"
What did you just say?

Cary was obviously as surprised at the offer as Heath.

"Uh, no. No we couldn't put you out like that. He's a good kid, but... he's a kid and I'm sure he'd get in the way."

"It wouldn't be a big deal. Not like he doesn't

know me." *What are you doing?*

Cary looked back out at the water thoughtfully. "He would love it. We could come on a Saturday after feeding the dogs. Doggies and boats in one day. He'll be beside himself." Cary laughed, mostly to himself. He had a gentlest smile on his face, one that gave Heath the urge to both hug him and toss himself overboard.

"Well, I'm off on my two weeks so next weekend, I guess."

"Only if you're sure."

Yeah, strangely he *was* sure. For now, he'd just let himself think it was because he couldn't disappoint the kid.

Cary turned an unusually saucy look Heath's way. "I think you just earned yourself some benefits, *friend.*"

Well, I'll be damned. "Well, hell, if I'd known that'd keep you coming back I'd've offered sooner."

Cary snorted, but moved to straddle Heath, both of their bodies responding to the other, rocking and growing heated. "Don't overuse the kid card. I can separate the bullshit from sincerity."

"Noted."

"Now. I think it's my turn to taste you." And Cary went to his knees.

Chapter 6

"I don't know what I'm even doing," Cary complained, banging his head on the desk in Celine's office. She laughed musically as she tapped on the keyboard to her computer.

"You are having good sex," she said in her flirtiest voice, French accent lilting just so. Cary couldn't help the giggle that caused. No doubt about it, she was right. She considered herself his personal love guru at this point. If he got a message from Heath, she was shooing him out the door. He'd only taken her up on it once more in the week since Heath had come home, and they'd had more mind blowing sex. Cary had never been with someone quite so toppy and it could easily become an addiction for him.

But Heath was also good company. After last time they had sex, they'd once again spent a while just talking about nothing of importance, drinking a beer, and enjoying looking at the ocean. He'd never felt quite so free as he did enjoying his friendship with Heath. He was a little bummed it couldn't go any further, but he understood Heath's reasons. And Heath was a nice guy. But seriously...

"I'm taking my child to hang out with my fuck buddy."

"Stop being ridiculous. He is a nice man and you are not introducing him as anything other than a friend. Gus already knows him, anyway. It's not like you are always with a new boyfriend, rotating man after man in front of him."

He snorted. "No doubt. This is the first person he'll ever be around that I've even kissed."

"Which has not been many since *that man* left." *That man* being Marshall. She'd actually met Cary through Marshall, his veterinary clinic being the shelter's go to clinic until he'd up and left town. And Cary. She had swooped right in, offering to rent him the other half of her duplex. She'd been angry for her animals being abandoned, and having grown so close to Cary, was fierce in her anger on his behalf as well.

"You're right. But I should really back off. He has become someone I talk to, a friend of sorts. I should stop with the benefits part because I really suck."

A mischievous smile curled her lips. "Is that not the point?"

Cary guffawed, tossing a dog treat at her. "That's not what I meant. I meant I have a crush."

"Well, you're a grown up. You're allowed to enjoy yourself so long as it is not affecting the well-being of your child, and you are so very responsible with him. There is no harm in enjoying this crush so long as you remind yourself it will go no further than that. You are a smart man. Don't over think."

She was right. He was being ridiculous. He certainly wasn't in love and Lord knew Heath may be a go to guy for good sex and beer at the beach, maybe a night at the bar with buddies, but you didn't marry guys like Heath. Heath worked hard so he was rarely home, and played harder so he wouldn't stay home. And Cary had to admit, the whole bisexual thing was still a niggle for him. He hated feeling that way, but any time Heath mentioned a woman he'd previously been with, Cary felt a little burst of anxiety. He knew it was for no good reason and he didn't think being bisexual made the guy some sort of cheating jerk. But it was an insecurity on his part, plain and simple.

And why was he even worrying about whether the guy was cheating, be it with woman or another man? Nothing about what they were doing was exclusive.

"Daddy! Look!" Gus's voice brought Cary's attention back to where he was. His son and Celine's daughter Savannah were coming in from the kennels. They both looked far worse for wear, sweaty and dirty. Cary had no idea how Savannah was wearing her usual black jeans and black t-shirt and not melting when it was over a hundred degrees outside.

Gus toddled over to the chair Cary was sitting in and struggled to climb in his lap. Cary knew better than to assist, though. Gus was at that stage where he'd get the old, "No daddy, I do it."

"He just had to come show you," Savannah drawled. Typical teenager, put out by the heat and being run to death by Gus. She could put on all she wanted, they all knew she adored the little boy.

"What you got there?" Cary asked when Gus had finally settled on his lap. He held out his hands and waited for Savannah to settle a newborn puppy in his hands. Gus was thrilled with the little thing. Cary helped him hold it, reminding him to be gentle. After a few moments of discussing how they could not take the puppy home, and getting an angry glare from one disgruntled toddler, Savannah offered to take the puppy back to the kennels.

"That's a cute little guy." Cary'd recognize that

voice anywhere. It licked him from head to toe, deep and warm. He looked up, smiling at Heath. He'd been out in the kennels helping with the heavier lifting. Gus had actually deigned to speak to the man a few times since Cary'd told him they'd be going to see 'Heaf's' boat today. Heath pulled off the sweaty, dirty look well. His bronzed skin glistened while his sun bleached hair looked airy and refreshed. His arms were amazing in the sleeveless shirt and Cary really wanted to reach up and just squeeze a bicep.

Heath winked at him, it being plain that Cary was checking him out. Busted.

"You can take him home then," Cary said.

"Ah, no dogs. I really would love to, but two weeks on, two weeks off is not conducive to pet ownership. I'd love to one day, though."

"Oh, I meant the kid. Me and Celine can go for drinks. It's hot."

Heath looked momentarily horrified at the thought before cocking a brow. "You two have been sitting in the air conditioning the last half hour. I don't know what you're complaining about."

"You boys can take your flirting right out of my office," Celine said, smirking. "Don't you have a play date or something?" Cary glanced at Heath whose expression was what he imagined they were talking about in romance novels when they said 'rakish'. Cary couldn't stop his grin when he thought how hot it was he'd put that look on Heath's face.

"Boat!" Gus said. Yeah, he wouldn't let anyone forget what they were supposed to be doing today.

"Right," Cary said, turning back to Celine whose smile was positively smug. He rolled his eyes at her. "Yes, Gus has a play date with Mr. Heath today."

"Mr. Heaf has a boat," Gus said happily to Celine.

"Yes, a very messy boat," Heath said. Cary quirked an eyebrow.

"Sorry," Heath said, shrugging. "I ran a charter last night for some people I'm trying to get to sign a contract— You don't care about all the business talk. So if you guys can hang back about thirty minutes, Kyle and I should have all the mess cleared out."

"Sure thing," Cary said, giving him an understanding smile. "I appreciate you taking us out today."

Heath dipped his head. "Not a problem. It's good anyway. Wouldn't want the munchkin to burn. Give the sun some time to move out." He then gave a report to Celine as to what he'd gotten done that day and headed out.

"Oh, chéri," Celine said with a wistful sigh. "I do believe you are not the only one with a crush." At Cary's scoff she smirked. "I have known that man many years. I can say I've honestly never seen him so..." She looked thoughtful, using her slender hand to wave like she was searching her mind for something. Then she looked at him evenly. "Satisfied."

Cary scoffed again. "Anyway... I think me and the boy should help Savannah finish up out there, since we have time to kill." He set Gus back on his feet and patted his rear to get him to move.

"Go find Savannah," he said. Gus bounced a couple times, then asked, quite seriously, if they'd still be going for a ride on the boat. Cary gave an equally solemn reassurance which appeased his son enough to have him running out and calling for Savannah.

"Going on a boat!" Celine and Cary both laughed at the excited proclamation Gus made when he'd found 'his Savannah'.

"That one will be trouble one day," Celine said, laughing.

"*Will* be?"

Celine waved him off. "Now he is sweet and loving. You are in for trouble when he stops with the quiet and the minding of manners."

Cary groaned. "Please, let's not talk about it. I'm not ready for him to get any bigger." He looked through the window in the door, watching Gus help Savannah in the kennels outside, talking excitedly with his hands. Cary had been the one that didn't want children, too young for the commitment, too fun-and-fancy-free. Now he loved the boy so much he just couldn't fathom a day when the pint-sized love of his whole life would be tired of him.

"Cary, be careful." *What?* Cary's attention snapped back to Celine, trying to catch up.

"Be careful of what?"

"I said he has a crush, I know you have one. But you know him as he is now. I have known him much longer. Heath will not settle down. Once bitten, they say."

"Oh, yeah. I know about the ex-wife and all."

Her expression was dubious. "You will be careful, no? I know I say it is okay to fall in love, but remember to do it with the right man."

"Love? Who said anything about that? I barely have time to sleep with the guy, much less date and/or fall in love with him."

"If you say so," she said, doubtfully, turning

back to her computer. "Now, out. If I want to have any sort of day off tomorrow, I must finish." He laughed when she started shooing him so he went to help the kids with the final feedings.

Love. He scoffed to himself. Who had time for love? Yeah, while it'd be nice to find someone, not only for himself but for Gus, he had no illusions that Heath would be that man. Heath was the 'cool uncle' sort, the one who did fun things with Gus, was friends with daddy and his partner, but didn't do twenty-four-seven parenting. He was the guy that got you off, gave you a beer and an ear, then sent you back to real life. There was no point in even fantasizing about more. And Lord knows the perks were just what he needed right now, so no way was he going to get attached and scare the guy off.

****

Cary held Gus's hand as they walked down the now-familiar docks of the Santa Rosa Dock & Marina, where Heath's yacht was berthed. Gus chattered on, oohing and aahing over the boats they passed. Cary could hear Heath's correction in his head each time. *"It's a yacht. A boat is that thing your grandfather uses when he fishes in a pond."*

When they rounded to where Heath's boat was docked, Cary noticed him talking to a man in a cheesy boat captain's uniform. It wasn't until they got right up to the pair, he realized it was Heath's friend from the bar, Kyle. Kyle turned with his biggest, most lecherous smile. Even in his costume—no way he was expecting anyone to buy that was a real uniform—the man was sinfully hot. He had a similar build to Heath, while being a few inches shorter than Heath who was easily eye-to-eye with Cary. He thought he remembered Heath saying something along the lines of them having served in the Coast Guard together, though Kyle was probably more Cary's age than Heath's. He honestly didn't look much older than your average baby faced frat-boy, though, and had the mischievous glint in his eye to match.

"Damn, Heath. You didn't tell me we had a hottie coming by."

Heath gave his friend a shove from behind, making Kyle laugh. Cary chuckled but tipped his head to point out Gus. "Tiny human alert." Kyle's smile went from lecherous to disarmingly kind as he took a knee, getting eye level with Gus.

"Wow," Gus said reverently. "You drive a boat?"

"Yes sir, I do. Captain Kyle at your service." He

held out a hand but Gus, in his true shy nature, remembered he didn't know the man and moved back a step and sideways behind Cary.

"You driving today?" Gus asked.

Kyle shook his head with exaggerated sadness. "No, not this time. I have to take a bunch of old guys out fishing. But Heath over there is going to take you. He's okay, but I'm better so I'll have to take you next time." Kyle tilted his head and gave Cary a wink. Cary snorted and gave Heath a grin.

"You're going to be *late*, Kyle," Heath said, tone dripping with exasperation.

Kyle took his hat off and put it on Gus's head. "Hold that until I see you next time, little man." He got to his feet and held up his hands at the glare he was getting from Heath. "I got it, I got it. Hint taken. I'm out." He started walking, winking at Cary again. "Y'all don't do anything I wouldn't do."

Cary laughed. "Do people still say that?"

Heath grunted. "He's a brat."

"Oh, yeah. The young whippersnapper must get on your nerves," Cary teased.

"That's why I give him all the BS clients," he said with a wink.

Gus started tugging on Cary's hand. Cary picked

him up and got a put-upon sigh for his effort. "What's up Gus?" he asked.

"Can we go now?"

Heath laughed and directed them to the boat. After they'd gone aboard, Heath took over instructing Gus on how to put on his life-jacket. Gus wasn't thrilled with the bulky thing but he didn't try to take it off after Heath tightened the straps for him.

"I figured I'd take you guys for a quick spin so he can be on the yacht, maybe take her about thirty minutes down, hit Mexico Beach and let him hang out over there. He can't fish, too young, so I hate to rip him off not making an afternoon of it."

"I thought you weren't good with the kid thing."

Heath gave another grunt as he dropped a life-vest over Cary's head and snapped it on. "It seems to be a cosmic joke the universe has played on me. I'm good with kids, they like me... I just don't want 'em. Now hold your arms out." Cary complied, letting his proverbial balloon deflate and spin to the ground after that swift popping. *What was it Kyle said? Hint taken.*

"You know, I'm pretty capable of putting on my own vest."

Heath leaned in, breath ghosting over Cary's ear as he spoke in a rumbling, sexy drawl. "Gotta touch you how I can, when I can."

Cary shivered. "Not fair," he said. Heath pulled back, smirking. Cary scowled playfully then asked where he and Gus should sit.

"Come in the cabin for now, buckle in. He'll be able to see great out the panoramics."

They followed Heath inside and got buckled in while he checked a million things. When he started the yacht, Gus gave an excited giggle that made Cary's heart pitter-patter. He loved seeing his son happy, and he'd have to thank Heath properly for putting that smile on Gus's face.

As they made the trip toward Mexico Beach, Gus asked a million questions which Heath answered patiently. Cary was impressed. The man didn't speak to Gus like he was a little kid, but gave complete answers, explaining things Gus may not understand. Gus was enraptured. Cary would be lying to himself if he said he wasn't as well.

After they made it to the beach, Heath pulled out hot dogs and sodas. Cary couldn't even fuss about the sugar because Gus was having such a great time. He hadn't stopped smiling once. And for Gus, that'd be a record. He was often a serious, quiet child. Only when he made new discoveries or had gotten so dirty Cary wanted to cringe would he smile as much as he had today.

They docked and walked up the beach for a minute. Heath and Cary helped Gus pick out shells. Cary had never been to this particular beach. It wasn't the same pristine white sand as their part of the panhandle, it was more rocky and shell-covered. It was Gus's dream beach. He had filled a Crown Royal bag Heath had provided. *He would give a three year old a whiskey bag.* Heath had just shrugged at Cary's raised eyebrow when he'd pulled it out.

After they'd gone back to the boat, everyone donned life-vests again and they'd put out a blanket on the deck. Heath explained what each shell was to them, more to Gus than Cary, but Cary didn't mind because with their attention being held by the shells he could watch the way they interacted. He also used the opportunity to steal several looks at Heath, who occasionally would glance up at him and smirk.

"Daddy! Look! Wow! Oh, wow!" Cary jumped at Gus's exclamation. He'd nearly swallowed his tongue when his son ran to the rails and tried to climb up the side to look over. Heath was right on the boy, though, slipping his hand inside the collar of his life-vest to hold him firm. Cary let out a sigh of relief. When he stood to check what had Gus so excited, he could see dolphin fins sliding through the water about a hundred yards out. He'd seen dolphins about a hundred times since he'd moved to Florida but this was probably a first for Gus.

Cary was about to join them at the railing when he came up short. Heath had knelt down so he and Gus were on the same level and was pointing at the dolphins. They spoke quietly to one another, heads tilting first to one side then the other in unison as they watched the dolphins swimming and playing. Cary's heart swelled in his chest. God, he needed to be careful. The sight of Heath and Gus together like that made him weak in the knees and that was dangerous.

Then they both turned to him with matching smiles. The air left his lungs as he took in their exuberance, the twin gleams in their eyes. Now he understood why Celine had told him to be careful. He'd just had a crush before, but now... now he realized how easily he could fall for Heath. And Lord did that realization suck.

He shook himself out of his thoughts and walked over to stand by them, watching the dolphins. But he couldn't stand it anymore. Thankfully the sun was almost gone from the sky, leaving him watching the sunset with Heath yet again, with its pink and orange hues. Damn, it'd been a good day.

"We should get going, huh?" Heath asked, hand landing on top of Cary's where it rested on the rail. Cary looked at the weathered, work calloused hand.

"Yeah," he said thickly. "Probably a good idea."

On the way back, Gus asked if he could help drive. It was probably against the rules but Heath had allowed him to. He went on and on about the dolphins for the first twenty minutes of the ride while Heath murmured agreements. Cary just watched as the sun disappeared and the water grew dark. As they slid through the night, Gus grew silent. Cary glanced toward them to see Gus had fallen asleep in Heath's lap. Heath was humming something quietly to himself, or maybe to Gus. Cary felt a knot form in his throat and offered to take Gus from Heath.

"He's fine," Heath said peacefully. Cary just nodded and stared at them until they were back in the dock in Pensacola Beach.

"Okay, now you can take him," Heath said. "I have to go handle the mooring, check things out." He thought he heard a catch in the man's voice, but he looked as passive as ever so Cary just took the precious bundle he was being passed and started taking off Gus's life-vest.

When Heath came back in the cabin, he stood quietly watching Cary and Gus. "Let him sleep."

Cary glanced Heath's way, a question in his eyes.

"Give him a minute. I'm sure he's tired."

Cary nodded slowly, laying Gus out on the cushioned bench. He walked over to where Heath stood and did something he'd been dying to do all afternoon—kissed him. It was soft and light, not demanding anything, just a thank you. Heath's hand wrapped behind Cary's head, carding his fingers through Cary's hair.

Heath smelled good as ever, sunshine and light sweat, citrusy and free. Tongues never joined in, but they weren't necessary. Just the lightest sucking on Heath's bottom lip and vice versa. Heath's hand slipped around Cary's waist. When the kiss ended Cary whispered a "Thank you."

"It was no problem. I had a good time."

"Gus loved it. You were awesome with him."

"He's a cool kid."

Cary smiled, knowing all the adoration he had for his son was showing on his face. "Yeah, he is that." He pulled back enough to see Heath's face. "You never wanted kids?"

Heath's face scrunched up. "No way. Almost had one once." He pulled away. "That's why me and the ex got married. Teenage mistakes are the worst reason to take that plunge."

"I don't doubt it."

"It worked out for the best, though. She got her career, we got out of the most miserable marriage ever. Of course, sometimes I wonder what it would have been like to have a little guy like yours, but I think it saved us from more heartache down the line. And proved I just am not father material." Cary didn't want to talk about that any more than he wanted to talk about the ex-wife.

Cary turned to look at Gus. "I never thought I was, but when Marshall took off, I had to do it. I don't regret it, but no doubt it wasn't easy."

"What happened? If you don't mind me asking?" Heath looked surprised, like he hadn't meant to ask, suddenly fidgeting and uncomfortable.

"Well, he wanted the surrogate. I was just twenty-four going on twenty-five. He was thirty-one and we'd been together four years. Now that his clinic was going well—he's a vet—he thought it made sense. Until his sperm wouldn't do anything and we decided to try mine before going the more expensive in vitro method. After a couple tries, Gus happened." Cary sighed, remembering how much the next part of the story hurt. But enough time had passed since then, and he'd gotten Gus, who he'd never give up. He wouldn't change it for anything.

"He seemed more miffed than excited when it happened. By the time we got five months into the pregnancy and he was increasingly weird about it. When the ultrasound showed we were having a boy, Marshall said he was too jealous, resentful. He wanted his *"own"* son. He couldn't handle the baby not being biologically his and he left. *"So I won't hate you and the kid"*."

"That's the stupidest shit I've ever heard," Heath snapped.

Cary turned to him, surprised. "Yeah. It sucked, but what could I do? Some said I should give Gus up. The surrogate was willing to help find a couple. But he was mine, y'know? I'd already gotten excited to have *our* child. I couldn't just... walk away. I guess I still don't get how he could."

"Well, why'd he want you to try if he never wanted your kid? Seems like he didn't think of it as being *y'all's* kid unless it was conceived with his sperm." Cary wished he could explain it. He was just as confused as Heath.

"I honestly don't know. It didn't matter to me who the biological father was. He'd have always been ours. Heck, I still let his dad see Gus whenever he wants. Marshall's never tried, though. I've always wanted to ask him why he didn't just go with in vitro fertilization in the first place if the baby being conceived with my DNA was going to be such a problem for him."

Heath put a hand on Cary's shoulder and when their eyes met he saw sympathy there. "That's a tough break. But you and Gus made out alright, huh?"

Cary sighed contentedly as Heath placed a brief kiss on his lips. "I guess things work out as they're supposed to. I'm happy, he's healthy." Heath studied Cary closely before clearing his throat and going back to his typically passive, macho posture. Cary resisted rolling his eyes. First, he was trying to break the habit so Gus wouldn't pick it up, second, he guessed he shouldn't have been surprised. He couldn't let himself forget that this was what it was. Heath was his friend, his occasional fuck. Nothing more, nothing less.

"Well," Cary said, taking a few steps back. "I better get Gus home." Heath merely grunted, causing

Cary to sigh inwardly. "Thanks again for today."

And with that, he gathered up his son and left the boat—and Heath. He wondered, momentarily, if he would ever come back. He figured the shuttered expression Heath gave him when they'd kissed goodbye was his answer to that question.

Better to end this, whatever it was, sooner rather than later. God knows he didn't need to get any more attached and, like a major dummy, that seemed to be exactly where he was heading.

Chapter 7

Heath stretched out on a towel on the bow of the *Keep Swimming*. This was the life, indeed. Right? *Of course. Everyone wants this life.* He took a chug of his Dos Equis and set the bottle down, probably a little more heavy handed than necessary. He loved his life. He could do without the backbreaking work, but on his two off he didn't answer to anyone, had a business that was his dream, good friends and good beer. He lived on a fucking yacht for fuck's sake. He was a walking, talking beach-bum bachelor cliché minus a surf board.

Much to his mother's chagrin, he loved not having someone back home to worry about while away for work. He loved returning to his own space, free to do his own thing, fuck who he wanted. So why, *why* was he suddenly hung up on Cary Whitmore and his kid? He didn't even want kids, sure as hell not twenty-four hours a day. *"Sometimes things work out how they're supposed to."* Cary had said. He couldn't imagine he'd gone through all that shit, the miscarriage and shitty marriage, to end up saddled with a kid anyway.

Because being with them was such a burden.

Heath scowled, even his own thoughts were mocking him now. He took another draw, finishing off his beer then raised up on one elbow, leaning to grab another bottle from the bucket he'd brought outside.

"Captain Kyle requesting permission to come aboard!" The yacht dipped as Kyle boarded. Heath shook his head. Kyle appeared after a few seconds, stretching out beside him and snatching a beer for himself. "Yo, ho, ho!"

"You're in a good mood," Heath said, eyeing his friend briefly.

"Why wouldn't I be? Finally got those bastards from Conklin to give us a shot at bidding for their seasonal contracts."

That made Heath *very* happy. They'd been after a contract like that since they'd started up. It'd be one more step toward him getting off the damn rigs.

"Question is, with that piece you've got on tap, why aren't *you* in a good mood?"

Heath grunted. "There is no piece on tap."

"Oh, so we're defensive over him. My bad. He's not a piece," Kyle said placatingly.

"I didn't mean it that way. I mean, we're finished with the fucking around."

"Seriously?" Kyle sounded genuinely surprised, so Heath peeked his friend's way.

"Why is that surprising?"

"Well, dude he's hot. And you took his kid out. You've fucked around with people with kids before and not taken their kids out. I just thought maybe..."

Heath grunted again. He seemed to be going that a lot lately. "He was just a friend. Now I'm backing off the fucking. Didn't want it to get heavy."

"Oh, please. You don't *do* heavy. I forgot."

"Why would I?" Heath asked, sitting up and drawing from his beer. "Not like I can date him. He's out. I can't fuck with that right now. Plus, with my schedule I can't even have a dog, how would I date?"

"I'm sure he'd appreciate being compared to a dog."

Heath glared at his friend. "You know what I mean, you little shit."

"I'm hearing reasons you can't be in a relationship. Usually you'd be giving reasons why you don't want to give up being a bachelor, is all."

Heath stilled. He hadn't thought of that. He'd been so busy coming up with reasons he couldn't date *Cary*, while forgetting he didn't want to date *anyone*. He was a bachelor. Wait.

"No. I just was thinking how much I don't want kids. I was thinking also, why would I want someone I'd have to answer to? Someone freaking out because I'm gone two weeks at a time, in my face all the time over my schedule."

"Yeah. Why on earth would you want a hot guy sitting at home, patiently waiting for you to dick him down, while worrying about your well-being?" Kyle was squatting next to him when he put his hand on his chest, eyes going comically wide. "The horror!"

Heath shoved his friend, making him topple over. When he hit the ground he had the nerve to laugh for a minute, kicking his legs and giggling like a little kid. "You're a dumbass."

Kyle sat up and gave him a sardonic look. "You're one to talk, douche." He sat down, crossing his legs and looked up at the sky. "Oh!" he said, surprising Heath who looked at him like he'd lost his damn mind. *What mind did he have to lose, honestly?*

"So, now you're done with him, do you mind if I hit that?"

"What?" Heath asked, drily.

"I mean, we've shared before, right? Hell, you've fucked *me*. He's hot." He cut his eyes toward Heath, boyish mischief flashing in their green depths. "I've always thought I'd make a good step-daddy."

Heath sat up, quickly, pointing a finger in Kyle's face. "Back. Off. Y'hear me?"

"Touchy, touchy." Kyle brushed imaginary lint from the shoulder of his sleeveless shirt. "One might say you were..." He leveled Heath with his gaze. "Jealous."

Heath's mouth opened, closed, opened, closed.

"You're jealous!" Kyle said, pointing with both fingers. He jumped to standing and did his annoying I-told-you-so victory dance. Oh, shit. Was Kyle right? There had been a blind fury that swept through him when Kyle said he'd wanted to hook up with Cary. It had gotten even worse when he said he'd try to be a part of Gus's life.

Heath's mind flashed back for the hundredth time in the four days since he'd taken Cary and Gus out—four days since he'd responded to Cary's attempts to contact him or even attempted to contact Cary himself—and all he could ever think was how he'd had one of the best days of his life with the Whitmore boys. It'd been so simple, laid back with no expectations. They both just *fit* in Heath's life, even if it had been for just five minutes, and when it'd been time for it to end Heath had been saddened. Then he'd freaked out and sent them on their way, hoping time and space would rid him of the fact he was starting to care for them.

When Cary had talked about his ex abandoning them, he'd wanted to find the guy and break his legs them come back and take these precious gifts the stupid man had tossed aside and make them his own.

But. No. He couldn't.

Two hands were suddenly on his face, Kyle's bright green eyes boring into his as he straddled Heath's lap. "Stop being a dumbass."

He jerked his head back. "What are you—"

"Oh shut up. You like him. You *never* like people. You maybe fuck 'em a couple months, maybe less, let 'em know the score, then it's over. You don't get involved. You're involved this time. Why not enjoy it?"

"Because you're such the relationship guy."

Kyle scowled. "I *try*. I'm not all allergic to relationship cooties. I just suck at the longevity part. But that's more than you. If nothing else, Heath, try. You've never *tried*."

"I did too! Remember the ex-wife?"

"Shut up with that, dude. Remember, I'm friends with her too. You never even told her you loved her. She was the same kinda fuck buddy as the rest, you just fucked up and knocked her up. This time, maybe it's a real chance."

Heath couldn't deny any of that. Was Kyle right? Could he try? It's not like he'd have to flaunt the relationship in front of the guys at work. Plus, he only had one more year, maybe a little more, to make enough to leave the rigs. That wasn't even long enough to have to worry about 'officially' being a couple.

"Maybe," he said to no one in particular.

"Maybe my ass," Kyle said, huffing.

"He'll be pissed at me, anyway. I haven't spoken to him in days. I've ignored him."

"Flowers."

Heath looked at his friend with his best 'what are you talking about' expression.

"Flowers. They work, trust me."

"Even with guys?" Heath asked, skeptical.

"Because *I've* been with women?" Kyle's scrunched up nose told what he thought of that idea. Heath laughed. No, not Kyle. Gay as they came, his Kyle. He'd been discreet when they were in the Guard, pre-DADT repeal, but he'd always been out in his own way, his personality much too wide-open to lie outright about anything. He'd not served more than his first four years with the Coast Guard, though. He'd mostly needed the money for college, which he'd finished in time to help Heath run his charter service.

"I guess I could try." He wasn't sure why he was being so agreeable. Maybe Kyle was right and he *was* tired of being alone. Maybe he'd never had anyone worth trying for. There was something about Cary Whitmore. It was like he'd found so many of the things he wanted in a partner in one person for the first time in his life. And he hadn't even thought he wanted a partner! It was, unfortunately, his biggest fear realized, he'd find those compatible, addictive traits in a man when it was still inconvenient for it to happen with a man. But Heath knew, above all, nothing worth having was ever easy.

"Go." Kyle snatched the beer out of Heath's hand and finished it. "Now." He grabbed the last beer and stretched out on his back. "I'll stand watch over your girl while you're gone."

"Of course you will." Heath shook his head. He jumped up and made his way in the cabin and into his room. He had no idea what he'd even wear.

He caught his reflection in the mirror above his sink. "You're really gonna do this, huh?" Yes, he was going to do this. It felt right. Weirdly right. Now he just hoped he hadn't fucked up too badly by ignoring Cary.

****

He decided to forgo the flowers, especially when he realized he was going to have to go to The Barkery to see Cary. He hoped that wasn't a serious misstep but he needed to do this now while he had the balls. If he sat around and thought on it any longer he'd talk himself out of it. And when he'd called Celine she'd said he was at work. "All the better to corner him, chéri."

He'd laughed, thinking maybe she was right. At his house he could slam the door in Heath's face. Of course, thinking that made Heath nervous. What if cornering him in his business was the easiest way to make him lash out? Why should he risk it? *Fuck, this is stupid.* He gripped the steering wheel and looked up at the windows of the bakery. He could see in, Cary was smiling at a woman who was ordering, holding her dachshund in her arms. This was a bad idea.

Then Cary's gaze landed on Heath and his smile flickered before he turned back to the woman at his counter. *Shit.* He couldn't just leave now could he? God, he'd not been this nervous about asking his first girlfriend to prom or the first time he blew Mason

James the summer before senior year. What the hell was going on with him? He saw what he wanted, took it. The end.

He jumped when there was a knock on his passenger side window. He looked to see Cary standing there, expression full of concern. Heath breathed deeply in and out and pressed the button to unlock the doors. Cary stood for a beat longer before opening the door and sitting down in the passenger seat.

"You okay?" Cary asked.

"Yeah. Feeling kinda ridiculous, actually."

"How so?"

He sighed and turned in his seat to look at Cary. "I'm sorry."

Cary's brows shot up. "For what exactly?"

"For not calling you. Or responding to you."

Cary looked down at his lap and started fiddling with the hem of his mint green 'The Barkery by the Bay' apron, shrugging. "Hey, we always knew the score. I was mostly calling to thank you again."

Heath reached out, placing a hand on Cary's forearm. "We knew the score. But... what if the score changed?"

Cary's head snapped in Heath's direction. "What do you mean?"

"I've been trying to think of how to talk to you about this the whole drive here and... well I guess I should just say it, huh?" Heath laughed self derisively. Cary's brow furrowed as he studied Heath dubiously. "I've had nothing but my boat and the hope to get off the rigs for so long I guess... I'm just surprising myself. Maybe it's because I'm getting older or somethin'. I don't know."

"You're not making much sense, Heath, and I have customers. Kent can't hold down the fort forever. Should we do this later?"

Heath shook his head vehemently. "No. No, I'm good. I've just never done this, okay? Hell, I never even dated my ex-wife, just got us in trouble and did what I was supposed to do when bad boys get good girls in the family way. We didn't even have a relationship. So I've gone thirty-two years without building any experience to fall back on." Cary let out a small sound of surprise when Heath wrapped a hand around the back of his neck and looked Cary in the eye. Those brilliant, hazel eyes with their specs of black and a ring of gray. Damn but the man had perfect eyes.

"I can't promise much, okay? My schedule is what it is, I'm horrible with children and I'm not out. But I'd love to keep seeing you and maybe let it turn into what it wants to on its own."

Cary stared, unblinking.

"Oh, shit." Heath sat back, extracting his hand. "Assuming you're looking for that. I didn't think about that."

Cary grabbed the hand Heath had just pulled away. "No, no. I do want that. I'm just surprised. Surprised you want to try and surprised you came here. Heck, I'm surprised you're so shy."

"I'm not shy," Heath grunted, shifting in his seat. Cary's face lit up and Heath knew he was in trouble.

"You so are. You're shy because want to keep me."

"Don't look so smug. You ain't catching some kinda prize. I'm gone two weeks at a time and we won't be able to see each other much more than we do now. I'm not ready to make any huge commitments or nothin'."

Cary's expression dimmed and he sat back in his seat. "Yeah, I get that."

Idiot. You gotta give something, here. He knew that much. "But I can promise I won't go fucking around on you. I'll let things play out." That seemed to perk Cary up a bit.

"What about Gus?"

"Uh." Heath knew he must look panicked because Cary laughed at him when he saw his expressions.

"Relax. I'm not trying to make you his other daddy or anything. But we are a package deal. So, maybe if we're gonna do this, you at least ... you have to be willing to accept that, and you'd have to respect that I have to pick him over you sometimes."

"I get that." He did. He'd never ask for anything different. "It's not like I won't fuck up and pick my career over you sometimes. I'm set in my ways. It won't be smooth sailing, but I'm willing to try."

Cary sat quietly for a long minute. Heath didn't know why he was holding his breath, why this was so important. But he finally exhaled when Cary turned that perfect smile, the one he'd grown addicted to, on him.

"Okay. Let's try. Just stop me if I ask something that's too much. But you *have* to talk to me. Even if it's to tell me we're not working. Okay?"

"I can do that," Heath said. Not that he was a master at communication but he could do that. He wrapped his hand around the back of Cary's neck again and kissed the man's smiling lips. God, he'd missed kissing this man. He didn't know what he was getting himself into, but what was life without at least trying?

Chapter 8

As Cary drove out to the marina he had to take deep breaths. In the two months they'd been seeing each other, two months since Heath had shown up and surprised the hell out of Cary by saying he wanted to *try*, Cary had gone through this a few times. The first night Heath would come home for his two weeks, Celine would keep Gus and Cary would meet Heath at the yacht. They'd spend the night having wild sex, sex that seemed to get better the more they figured out each others' bodies, sex that seemed to grow increasingly passionate.

They weren't by any means in a traditional relationship. They didn't get to see each other often, but they managed to text a lot. Heath would pop in for the surprise lunch here and there. They'd even taken Gus out on the boat again. But they didn't lie around whispering sweet nothings. Not that Cary assumed Heath would ever be the type. Cary didn't mind, though, because when Heath would hug him the first time after two weeks away, it was always a real, firm, I-missed-the-hell-outta-you hug.

When Heath whispered he'd missed Cary the first time, Cary almost fell off the bed. He knew Heath was in uncharted territory, and to be honest, Cary was also gun shy. He hadn't tried getting involved with anyone seriously since Marshall had walked out. He didn't want to fuck up and move to fast, nor did he want to push Heath. They were actually going at a pretty comfortable pace.

He just wished Heath talked a little more. They talked, of course. Talked about Heath's dream to run his charter service, funny stories from Heath's work on the oil rigs, talked about Gus; Cary was surprised at how fond Heath seemed to be of his son. They didn't really talk about the past much, though. He knew Heath was from Tallahassee, that he had a younger brother and he'd spent eight years in the Guard before leaving to work on the rigs. Heath knew most of the nightmare that was Marshall. Heath'd tried to talk about his ex-wife but it was uncomfortable enough for both of them that the conversation had been short-lived. Cary knew they were still friendly and she lived in Tallahassee, which was a comfortable distance in Cary's mind.

Cary figured that stuff would come over time, though. They were still finding their footing. They were both skittish. But they were trying. And it was early days, yet.

Cary's excitement grew when he pulled into the marina's parking lot and grabbed his book bag with his change of clothes and his Kindle out of the backseat. He was a little early, so Heath wouldn't be home yet. He thought he'd surprise him. He'd brought some carry-out and beer, since Heath was usually starved when he got home.

He boarded the *Keep Swimming* and groaned when he saw the door was unlatched. That meant Kyle was probably there checking up on things, his job when Heath was away. Sometimes Cary went out when Kyle was too busy to check in. That was the pretense he'd used when Heath gave him a key, which still made him giddy.

"Y'know, in case you need to get away for a minute. And you could water my plants. Or whatever." Heath mumbled most of it.

"You don't have plants, Heath."

"Well, I've never given someone my key, okay? So I don't know what I'm doing!" Heath's frustration had been adorable, and adorable was the last word Cary usually used for the big roughneck.

He kissed Heath. "Thanks."

"Is it weird?"

"It'd be weird if you'd asked me to move in, and maybe I'm reading too much into the key."

That panicky look crossed Heath's face and Cary laughed. "Don't worry, I'm reeling myself in. I do appreciate it, though." Heath grunted; fucking sexy grunted. Cary had to have the man one more time before he left.

Cary *had* been excited about tonight, but once Kyle saw food and beer he'd pretty much be sure to stick around a few hours. He thought cock-blocking was a funny game.

Cary went into the cabin and below deck to put away the beer and carry-out. He tossed his bag in Heath's bedroom. When he came out, someone called "Heath, that you, babe?"

Babe? A distinctly female someone calling Heath babe? *What. The. Fuck?*

Cary felt his eyes trying to bulge out of his head as he made the slow climb up into the cabin. A very pretty, very topless brown-haired woman stood at the door.

"Oh, shit!" she exclaimed, running back on the bow. Cary stood, blinking wildly, trying to assess the situation, but coming up sorely lacking in brain activity.

The woman came back in the cabin, bikini top back on, hair done up in a pony tail. "I'm so mortified," she said. Her lovely face was tinted red with embarrassment. "Heath didn't warn me someone might stop by."

"Um, it's okay?" *I'll be damned it's okay.* Irrational anger flooded him, jealousy roaring like a mean green thunder in his chest.

She held out a hand. "Sorry about that. I'm Becca."

"The wife, Becca?"

She tittered a laugh. "That'd be me." *Now would be the time to correct me; say ex-wife.*

"Cary," he said, eying her hand like it may bite. "Um, I should..." He pointed to the door and she cocked her head, confused. "Yeah..." he mumbled and headed out. He turned back and said to her, "Just tell Heath I was here."

"Um, alright," she drawled. How dare she sound so annoyed? Yes, he'd been rude, or something. But what the hell? His ex-wife? Just showing up out of the blue, naked like it was okay. Was this usual?

Cary pulled up in front of his house, not having remembered even driving home. He knocked on

Celine's door. Tonight's plans were obviously a bust. He was sure Heath would be too busy entertaining his ex-fucking-wife. Lord, he never cussed so much. He needed to calm down. But seriously?

Hurt bloomed in his chest. He knew he'd been expecting too much, getting too comfortable. They'd both said over and over that they weren't committed, but when Heath said he wasn't going to fool around with anyone else, Cary had expected that to mean anyone.

"What's up, Uncle Cary?" Savannah had opened the door and Cary hadn't even noticed. "I thought you were out with your guy?"

"Change of plans," Cary said bitterly.

"Okaaaay," Savannah drew out. "Want me to get Gus?" He just nodded. By the time he collected Gus and begged off dinner with the ladies, he'd calmed down considerably. He felt ridiculous. He'd been a dick to Becca. She'd seemed as surprised by his appearance as he was by hers. And dang it all, he'd left his bag over there. He was humiliated.

He knew they were still friends, and if he thought about it, he realized he shouldn't have been shocked she might also have a key. Heath had said she liked to vacation on the panhandle when she could. He hadn't expected it to be on Heath's boat, for sure, but that didn't mean Heath was sleeping with his ex-wife.

"Daddy okay?" Gus asked. Cary looked at his son who'd been sitting on the couch quietly watching a movie next to Cary while Cary pretended to thumb through a magazine.

"Yeah, buddy. Daddy's being silly." *Aren't you, though?*

"Daddy's silly," Gus said, laughing. Cary raised a brow wondering why that was funny.

"I think it's time for bed don't you?"

"Can I sleep wif you?" Cary snorted. Maybe it was time for a speech pathologist. The kid just could *not* master his T-Hs.

"Yes. You can. But brush your teeth first."

"Okay!" Gus had to roll on his stomach and touch down one foot at a time, still too small to get off the couch any other way. Cary laughed as he watched his son run down the hall. Gus had been exactly what he needed. Maybe tomorrow he could figure out how he felt about the rest of it. He felt ridiculous enough as it was, but he didn't know how to handle this new development, or how much right he had to feel offended in the situation.

Gus wandered across the hall into his bedroom

then came out, crossing into Cary's with a stack of books in his arms. Cary smiled then went to turn out the lights and lock up. Looked like he'd be reading tonight. Thinking, he was sick of; reading, he could handle.

****

Heath jumped at his phone when it started ringing. *Thank God.* It was finally Cary. He'd tried to call him twice the night before. Becca had told him some guy named Cary had come by earlier but had seemed to not be feeling well and had gone. He hoped nothing was wrong, his first fear being something had happened with Gus. Cary'd left so fast he'd forgotten his bag.

Heath hadn't been able to touch the carry-out or beer Cary had brought with him. He smiled thinking about the fact Cary had tried to surprise him. Things like that had Heath becoming more and more addicted to the other man. He'd been so excited to see Cary's smile, to kiss him, touch him, he'd been disappointed when he wasn't home. Then he'd been so freaked out by

Becca's message he hadn't had time to freak out about being such a teenager-with-a-crush about the man, or about how Becca had looked at him and his reaction to her message like he was crazy.

"Cary? Hello?" he asked when he answered.

"Hey," Cary said, barely audible.

"Are you okay? Becca said you stopped by but you hauled ass. You left your bag."

The other end of the line was quiet enough Heath had to check the phone to make sure they were still connected. "Cary? Are you okay?"

"You were worried?"

"Of course! Is it Gus? What's wrong?"

"You were worried," Cary said, sounding surprised.

"Of course I was, what do you think, I'm some kinda asshole?"

"That's actually exactly what I think."

Heath plopped down on the couch, gut-punched and not knowing why it hurt to hear those words from Cary. Maybe because he'd been trying so hard to not be an ass where Cary was concerned. How had he fucked up? "What?" he asked softly.

"Look, I feel ridiculous for getting mad. I guess I should have talked to you yesterday but I had Gus and forgot about my phone because I was freaking out like a major weirdo."

Heath chuckled to himself when he heard Gus called his father silly in the background on the other end of the call. He still didn't understand, though. "Cary, you told me to talk to you when I'm feeling like I'm fucking up. Well, I guess I'm feeling like I'm fucking up and I don't even know how."

"Your ex-wife was at the boat."

"So..."

Cary gave an exasperated sigh. "Look, I guess I trust that you weren't gonna do anything with her, but I still didn't like coming in and your ex-wife was practically naked and comfortable like it was an everyday occurrence." Cary's voice grew shrill on the last few words and Heath winced.

Shit. He hadn't really thought of that. "So you left because she was here?"

"Because she was there naked and I thought *'Oh, hey, she's waiting on him to come home for the same reason as me.'*"

"That's not fair, Cary."

"No," Cary sighed. "It's not. And of course once I thought it through I knew it wasn't but I'd already lost it. But you know I'm insecure about her and it makes me feel crazy because I feel like I know you well enough by now that it shouldn't."

"I'd hope we're getting to that point. I've told you, man, I'm not fucking around with anybody, even if I don't know what that means, being committed or in a relationship. You also know I'm bi so there are women in my past and it gets old you flinching so often." Not that Cary was the first gay man Heath had been with that had that reaction. It seemed to be a pretty general response from the gold star crowd.

"I know, I do. And in this case it's not that it was a woman, it's that it was your *ex*. Who has a key."

"Well, Kyle's an ex, of sorts, and he has a key."

Cary groaned. "Really, Heath, *now* you drop that one on me?" Heath winced, realizing that'd probably not been his best move ever.

"I'm sorry. I can't change my past, and I'd hope you'd respect that. I'm with you, I'm trying for you. I don't know what else to do. I haven't fucked my ex-wife since well before we divorced, twelve years, at the very least. And Kyle, you've met. That was also like seven years ago. I'm trying to be with you."

"I know. I do, I just... had a moment. I do trust you. It was just a... surprise."

"What do we do? I don't want this to end over

something out of my control."

"You don't? I mean, I'm glad to hear that but... God, I'm a freak. I mean, I'm still pissed. You could have warned me, Heath. I guess I just don't know what to say. I don't judge you for the past, I don't. I think I'd have the same problem if any boyfriend's ex had free run of his house, though."

"You want me to tell her she can't hang out here?" Could he even do that? They'd been friends since they were fifteen.

"I don't know why I even said anything," Cary said. "I feel guilty. She's your friend, and it sounds like I'm saying not to hang out with her and I don't want to be that guy. Shit. I don't know. Just... Look, I have to take Gus to the kennel. It's doggy day. Maybe we can grab dinner this weekend and forget this happened?"

"If you're sure."

"Definitely. I'm sorry again. I gotta go." And he disconnected the call. Heath had no clue what to do. He'd never been in a serious relationship so he'd never run into this issue. And the guilt coming from Cary was genuine, he'd felt horrible even suggesting Heath do something about Becca's dropping by. Could Heath? Should he? Did Cary have the right to even ask?

He dialed Becca, who'd gone home earlier that

morning because she realized he needed space while he anxiously fumbled around below deck, waiting on Cary's call.

"Heath!" she answered. "Did you hear from your friend?

"Yeah. I'm a little lost."

"Okay, why?"

"Do you have a minute?" he asked.

"Of course. I'm just doing laundry. What's going on?" He heard the slamming of a washing machine's lid and the running of water, waited for silence to signal she'd left the laundry room.

"That guy, I've been seeing him."

"Well, I assumed he wasn't just a friend. Although, I've not seen you get that worked up over a fuck buddy before."

"No," he said, frustrated. "I've been *seeing* him."

"Oh. Oh, Heath that's great!" He could practically see her doing her happy dance in his head. She'd been on his ass to settle down, or at least see one person consistently, forever. Then she went quiet. "Oh, shit!"

"Yep. Finally caught on?"

"Oh now I'm even more mortified. Fuckin'-A,

Heath. Why didn't you warn me, I would never have shown up without calling ahead!"

"So it's not out of line to ask for that?"

"No, you big dummy. Are you kidding. If I'd been in Cary's shoes I'd've clawed my eyes out. Heath, I was topless! He must think I'm such a slut," she sounded just as exasperated as Heath felt.

"No, he actually felt guilty for flipping out."

"You're such a dumbass. Currents rarely want the exes around, especially if it's new. I know *I* don't. Remember what a bitch I was to Philip when he asked his ex-wife to house sit while we went to the Keys?" Did he ever. She called Heath railing about it for hours and he hadn't gotten what the big deal was.

"Oh, babe," she said, almost condescending. "You've never had a serious boyfriend, or girlfriend for that matter, so this may come as a shock to you. People get jealous." Heath understood that, he'd seen his friends do it over the significant others, he'd even seen one or two of his hookups get that way toward him, but he'd never really been attached enough to feel like that. And no one had ever been a big enough part of his life to have a say in who or what he did.

"So..." he said.

"How would you feel if you went to his house

and he was having dinner with his ex?"

"He wouldn't," Heath said matter-of-fact. "The guy was not good people."

"Well, say they worked out their differences. Say the guy started coming by regularly and your boy—Cary, right?—gave him a key to his place." Heath imagined it. Cary did have a child he considered part Marshall's. If the veterinarian rolled back in town and became part of Cary's life again, if they got tight. Heath's blood pressure went up just thinking about the guy trying to weasel his way back in Cary and Gus's life.

"Ah, you're making your caveman grunts," she said, sounding too amused at Heath's expense.

"Okay, I get it. But... am I ready for this? I've been seeing him exclusively for three months, gave him a key, I'd be banning my best friend from my house."

"Oh, shut up. You wouldn't be banning me, just asking me to be respectful enough—and I'd want Cary to know I can do that if he's going to be part of your life—that I give you guys space until Cary knows me well enough to flaunt my tits in his adorable face, too. And you need to ask yourself if you're ready, babe."

Heath chuckled but sobered as he said, "I can't lose him yet. I don't know why, but him and his kid, they just fit somewhere I didn't know was empty."

"Oh, shit. A kid?"

"Yeah, shut up." She was silent for a moment, Cary thought he heard her sniffle. He knew she had hurt much more and for much longer than he had over the loss of their baby. "Becca?"

"No, I'm good. But Heath, if you are willing to take on his kid too... I think you have your answer right there. You hate kids."

"I don't hate—" He didn't even finish the thought. She was right either way.

"Just keep doing what you're doing. It seems like it's been working for you guys. And remember you have to give a little, okay? He's not asking for a ring, just for some space to grow and that's daunting under the shadow of an ex."

"Thanks, Bec. I should probably go now. I have to go apologize for being relationship challenged, yet again."

"Go get him, Tiger. And don't worry too much, I'm sure he thinks your fumbling around in all this is as adorable as I do." She laughed at his growl and disconnected. He rubbed his hands over his face. He wished he could start getting some of this shit right, he wasn't creative enough to keep coming up with new and imaginative ways of apologizing. He just hoped

Cary wouldn't give up on him, yet.

Chapter 9

"Hold on guys," Cary said to Kent and Celine. They'd come over to cheer him up. He'd intended to call Heath but they'd shown up right after Gus's fever had spiked so he hadn't had a chance. They were busy cooking dinner when someone knocked on the door.

His friends agreed with him when he'd told them he'd just let his insecurities get the better of him. Kent had been quick to say it was okay, though. It was new, not just the relationship but dating in general. And he was felling for Heath. Bad. So waiting for the other shoe to drop was only natural. It was time, though, to put down his arms, to just let it be what it would be. He'd been good at that before, so now he needed to remember that not everyone was like Marshall. It was going to be okay, even if they didn't wind up together in the end. He'd at least know he was capable of doing this, of being with someone else.

He pulled the front door open, and all his breath left him at once. Heath was standing on his front step, holding flowers, dressed in the same green shirt from the first time they'd fooled around, and khaki shorts that revealed his long, tanned legs. He looked good enough to eat. But his expression was pained, uncharacteristically demure.

"Those for me?" Cary asked, nodding toward the flowers. Heath held them out and Cary had to stop from laughing, not only at the contrition Heath showed, but the dirt dangling from the roots of what looked like daisies Heath had pulled from someone's yard.

"None of the good flower shops were open," he mumbled. "And Kyle said flowers were good for apologizing." Cary guffawed, earning a frown from his boyfriend. He grabbed the daisies, hauled Heath in by his shirt and kissed him soundly.

When withdrew from the kiss, he beamed at the pleased flush on Heath's face. "No more apologizing. We're good, okay?"

"Becca says I'm a dumbass and she's not gonna drop in like that anymore. Apparently I was supposed to have warned her and you."

Cary leaned his forehead against Heath's. "We're good. I promise. I'm sorry, too. I should have stuck around and talked to you." He pulled back. "I'm relearning this stuff, too. So I'll mess up sometimes.

I'm just glad... that we're okay?"

Heath smiled, and it was a real smile. There was no seduction, no smirk, just an honest-to-goodness, happy showing of teeth and smile lines around wizened eyes. "Definitely okay." Heath kissed him again. "Do you want to see if someone can watch Gus and go for that dinner tonight?"

Cary was always surprised when Heath asked to go out somewhere, knowing how much the man valued his privacy and tried to keep a lid on their relationship. He understood the need, and usually when they ate out they did it somewhere very casual and acted more like buddies than boyfriends, but the fact Heath tried in his own bumbling way was cute and made Cary feel special.

Cary closed his eyes. "I'm sorry," he apologized. "I can't. Gus has a fever and it took forever to get him down tonight." He opened the door wider so Heath could see the people gathered in the kitchen, which you could see directly into from where they stood. "Celine and Kent are here for dinner. You're welcome—"

"Heath!" Celine called, dropping her spoon on the stove. She told Kent something about watching the food she'd been cooking in the skillet and came bustling over, long skirt fluttering around her. Her face was stretched into a pleased grin as she bussed a kiss on each of Heath's cheeks. "It is so good to see you. Come, come in. You must eat. I made paella and there's enough to feed us all for a week."

Heath glanced at Cary as if asking for permission. Cary rolled his eyes and grabbed Heath, wrapping a hand around a thick bicep. "Come on. Please, we'd love to have you." He led Heath in and they all gathered in the kitchen. Heath and Kent shook hands. They'd seen each other a few times, Heath having come in The Barkery by the Bay a couple times in the months they'd been together.

"You boys playing nice?" Kent asked. Cary shot him a glare, Heath's face flushing. Kent and Celine snickered, enjoying the situation too much for Cary's liking. He turned and mouthed *Sorry* to Heath who just smiled and pulled him in for a quick peck on the lips.

"So sweet, you two. I always said you two would be perfect together," Celine said, haughtily.

"And when did you say this?" Cary asked, tone dry.

"Many times, I just say it to myself. They are perfect, are they not, Kent?"

"If they'd both stop being such nervous

freaks," Kent replied. Again, Cary glared at his friends. Heath grabbed Cary's hand and gave it a squeeze. This was a new side of Heath. He'd seen it more and more lately, but mostly in the privacy of Heath's yacht. He would touch, and hold. It was strange at first to see the big man slowly become a softy who couldn't keep his hands to himself. But Cary liked it. He thought the butterflies that had just burst in his stomach with Heath's touch would choke him. He kept his gaze on Kent and Celine who taunted each other, Kent telling Celine she was cooking the paella wrong.

Finally, the food was ready and they all sat down at the table to eat, something that only happened when the whole group was together. Cary was fairly lax about Gus eating at the coffee table and watching the History Channel— his favorite. Who could fuss at a kid for wanting to watch documentaries on the ancient Egyptians?

They sat joking, talking about nothing heavy. Celine brought out a bottle of wine while Cary checked that Gus was still sleeping. He let the others finish off the bottle so he'd be prepared if Gus needed something through the night. He noticed even Heath backed off after two glasses. The man could drink like a fish, so the gesture was not missed. Cary placed a palm on Heath's knee and squeezed. Heath looked at him, turning up one corner of his mouth in a goofy grin.

"Okay, this is getting too sappy for me. I gotta be up early, so I think I should go," Kent said.

"Thanks again for doing inventory tomorrow," Cary said as he got up to walk Kent out. Celine took dishes to the sink, which Heath insisted he'd wash.

"Then I shall make my exit as well. It was a long day with my best volunteer sick," she winked at Cary and kissed his cheeks. "Goodnight, Heath." She touched a finger to Cary's nose and was out the door in a gust of flowing skirts and bangling bracelets.

Cary walked into the kitchen where Heath was doing the dishes. He placed his cheek on Heath's back and wrapped his arms around his waist. "Thanks for coming over."

Heath turned in his arms and kissed his forehead. "Thanks for having me. I had a good time." Heath grabbed a towel from behind him and wiped his hands before wrapping his own arms around Cary's waist and kissing him soundly, the quickest slip of tongue. "I missed you."

Cary sighed contentedly and lay his head on Heath's shoulder.

"Did I say something wrong?" Heath asked.

"No, not at all. I'm just surprised. You're... different." He leaned up and looked over Heath's handsome features. "I guess this isn't what I expected from you."

"It's not what I expected from myself, honestly. I've never done this. Not even..." He grimaced.

Cary chuckled. "Not with your ex-wife?"

Heath nodded. "Like I told you, she was a friend before and we fucked up. We're from a small town. We did what we were supposed to do. We were never in a relationship, just doing dumb kid stuff. After we lost the baby, we stayed together for one reason or another. Me being in the Guard helped pay for her school, our parents were appeased so long as the 'D' word never came up. They kept pressuring for more kids. We could barely sit in the same room with each other, though. We went from being best friends one year to hating each other the next."

"That sounds rough." Cary hated even commenting. He was eating up every morsel of this random sharing, he didn't want to stop its flow. He was honored Heath was opening up to him.

"It was. I stopped coming home on leave and finally when she finished her undergrad we hadn't really even seen each other face to face in over two years so we got divorced. Our friendship immediately bounced back. But it made me wary of ..." He used a hand to motion between himself and Cary. "This. What if I had found a good friend and we fucked it up like that because we tried for more. I hated the idea of losing a friend."

"So you kept the ones you had close, and the fuck buddies at arm's length."

"You make me sound like a whore," Heath said, equally amused and annoyed at once.

"No way, Heath. I don't think that. I think you were single a long time. Hell, I was a slut in college. Being single comes with its perks."

A fire appeared in Heath's eyes as he grabbed Cary's ass with both hands and pulled him close, lips a hair's breadth apart. "Well, being with you comes with its perks." He closed the distance, kissing Cary thoroughly and dirty.

"Daddy," Gus said behind them. They parted quickly. Gus was rubbing his eyes, luckily oblivious to what they'd been up to. They stole a smile at each other before Cary picked Gus up.

"Feeling okay, bud?" he asked, placing a hand on Gus's forehead. He seemed to have sweated off some of the fever.

"Heaf," he said, pointing over Cary's shoulder.

"Yep. Heath is here. He wanted to make sure you were okay."

He held out his hands. "Want you," he said to Heath. Cary checked with Heath who seemed mildly alarmed but held out long arms to take Gus from Cary. Gus was small for his age but in Heath's arms he looked like a rag doll, he flopped there lazily like one, too.

"We'll go out on the boat soon, okay?" Gus asked, eyes sliding closed as Heath held him. Heath laid a cheek on top of Gus's head which was leaned on Heath's broad chest.

"Of course. Any time, man." Cary had to lean against the counter for a second, his breathing tricky as he watched Heath sway gently, rocking Gus while he stood, both of their faces serene. Gus hated strangers, was often painfully shy. It had taken months to get him used to his preschool teacher. But there he lay, obviously feeling safe with Heath. And this wasn't the first time Gus had fallen asleep in Heath's arms. Only this time, Heath seemed to be as content as Gus with the development.

"I'm, uh," Cary said, pointing down the hall. "I'm gonna go get the thermometer. You can just go sit on the couch."

He went down the hall to grab the thermometer. When he caught his reflection in the mirror he saw the goofiest grin on his own face. He covered it with one hand, trying to stop it, trying not to read too much into this.

Finally, he headed back down the hall. "We can just check his temp and put him—" He stopped, still smiling. Laid back with the recliner kicked open, Heath slept soundly, Gus on his lap.

"You bastard," Cary said. Not even a flinch from either of his guys. Yeah, he was so screwed.

Chapter 10

Cary's eyes fluttered open, foggy mind swimming back to consciousness. When he finally realized there was a pair of eyes staring at him, his heart stuttered. The affection pouring off Heath in waves was enough to make Cary want to sing—something no one wanted him to do.

"Hey," Heath said.

"Morning," Cary croaked. He cleared his throat before he spoke again. "And hey to you."

Heath lay his head on Cary's bare chest and burrowed, stubble scratching, wrapping a strong arm around Cary's waist and pulling him close. His thick, hard cock nudged against Cary's thigh. Heath hummed his pleasure against Cary's neck as he ground himself against Cary.

Heath had just come home from another two weeks off shore. These days were Cary's favorite. They'd been separated just long enough to be insatiable, and it was even better now that Heath had gotten more openly affectionate. Rather than jumping each other and fucking like rabbits, sometimes they just lay and rubbed off on each other, and holy shit if every once in a while Heath wouldn't let slip a sweet nothing. They were succinct and not very flowery, usually something along the lines of how much he'd missed this, but it was more than Cary had hoped for. And he found it much more sincere than any of the ramblings and snuggling of some of his previous boyfriends.

He almost felt like he was dreaming some days, but he never questioned it. He went into the relationship just like he had when he and Heath had started their fuck buddy arrangement, eyes wide open and heart light. He enjoyed it for what it was. There were no proclamations of undying love, though Cary was pretty sure he was a goner, and there were no promises other than they intended to keep seeing each other until it ran its course or turned into something else—and God, but it seemed like it was turning into something more.

Heath wrapped a hand around Cary's cock and gave it a good stroking. "Oh, damn, Heath," Cary said, thrusting into the grip.

"Love when I make you say dirty words," Heath rumbled in Cary's ear. He kept stroking, thrusting his own cock against Cary's thigh until Cary reached down and started stroking him. He gave one of his sexy grunts and his lips found Cary's, tongue sweeping into Cary's mouth as he rolled on top of him. They stroked each other and kissed like they'd never get to kiss again. Heath ran his other hand through Cary's hair then gripped it, tugging. Cary moaned into their kiss.

Their cocks bumped into each other clumsily, balls rubbing as they thrust into each other and stroked. "Cum for me, Cary. Come on," Heath said against Cary's lips, tugging his hair gently and exposing his neck. Heath licked a line from collar bone to behind Cary's ear.

"Oh, fuck," Cary sighed, feeling his balls roll in their sac. He loved the way their softest, most sensitive skin touched. He rocked his pelvis rubbing their balls together, getting an appreciative humph from Heath. Then he felt the final tingles approaching.

"Oh, oh I'm gonna cum," Heath said. "Cum with me. Fuck, fuck." And Heath's mouth was back on Cary's, their kiss fumbling and wet and messy. As soon as he felt the wetness of Heath's cum hit his stomach, Cary fell into his orgasm, spewing on his own stomach. Their loads mixed as Heath fell onto Cary, their pelvises still giving feeble, searching thrusts.

Finally, their breathing evened out and Heath kissed Cary's jaw. "Now that's what I think about all the time when I'm on that damn rig."

"Oh?" Cary asked. "Thinking about all those sweaty roughnecks?" Cary was definitely teasing and Heath knew it.

He punched Cary's shoulder playfully and rolled off onto his own side of the bed. "If you saw the guys I work with, you wouldn't even tease." Then he turned his head to look at Cary. "'Sides, I only got eyes for you, darlin'."

Cary guffawed. "You're such an idiot."

"So I've been told," Heath said, stealing one last kiss as he got off the bed and wandered, bare assed, into the bathroom. Cary enjoyed watching those large, firm cheeks bounce as he walked. Heath came back with a towel, wiping himself off then threw it at Cary.

"Want to catch a shower?" Heath asked.

Cary checked his phone after he'd wiped his hands and stomach. "Actually, we slept in. Dang." He sat up and grabbed his boxers off the floor. "I promised Celine I'd be back with the cake by noon."

"Cake?"

"We decided at the last minute to do a birthday party for Gus. It's never a huge to-do but Manny is coming up, Celine and Savannah, probably Kent." Cary pulled his t-shirt over his head and grabbed shorts out of the bottom drawer. *His* drawer. That still blew his mind a bit.

He felt for his wallet and happened to catch the fact Heath wasn't making eye contact, studiously digging in his closet. Cary smirked. "We just decided last week so I wasn't able to call you. But you're welcome to come if you'd like."

Heath glanced from the side of his eye. "Will there be cake?"

"And booze for the adults. But I understand. I know how you are with kids, so if you don't feel like it."

"I could pop by for a minute," Heath said, nonchalant.

"I'm sure Gus would love that," Cary said, wrapping his arms around Heath and kissing the nape of his neck.

"If you're sure," Heath said.

Cary's forehead fell to Heath's shoulder and he snickered into the skin there. "You like my kid. Just admit it," he teased.

Heath turned him around, eyes crinkling with mirth and kissed Cary. "He's not so bad, but don't tell anyone I said so."

Cary saluted him. "Your secret's safe with me. God knows, Kyle would tease you for weeks."

"Months," Heath said. "I'd never hear the end of it. I can hear all the jokes now about how whipped I am."

Cary titled his head and studied Heath for a moment. "Whipped, huh?"

Heath scrunched his nose and glared. "Don't go gettin' a big head or nothin', Whitmore."

"You like me, you want to kiss me," Cary sang.

Heath put a hand over Cary's mouth. "Don't you have a cake to buy?"

"Oh, no!" Cary said. He'd gotten so distracted, he'd put himself behind schedule even more. But it'd been worth it.

"Cary?"

"Yeah?"

"I'm in this as much as I think you are... you know..." Heath mumbled. Cary's face ached from the cheesy grin splitting it. He kissed Heath quickly. Yeah, it'd definitely been worth it to be a few more minutes late.

"Definitely in it." He grabbed his car keys. "Party's at 2:30. If you don't want domestic, bring beer. Manny's a beer-nazi." Cary snorted. "Well, I don't suppose I should call a German Jew a nazi..." He waved off the thoughts, catching the amused look on Heath's face. "Okay, I'm gone."

And with a peck to the cheek he was out. When he got to the car and started it up, it really sank in, Heath's words. *"I'm in this as much as I think you are."* That jerk would slip that in on Cary when he didn't have time to process it.

So the whole drive to pick up the cake, then the drive home, Cary did what he seemed to do every time he left that infuriating man. He smiled.

****

Heath's palms were sweating. He couldn't recall that happening many times in his life. He was confident when it came to being a proficient lover, he was good at his job, he liked to think he was a good friend. He didn't know yet, but he assumed he was being a good boyfriend to Cary, even if that had and was continuing to take some getting accustomed to. But he had never met anyone's family, nor had he done the 'family thing'.

He glanced at the beer and gift for Gus in the

passenger seat of his Jeep then back toward the line of cars in front of Cary's duplex. He knew all Cary's closest friends were gathered as one, and though it caused him a weird jealousy he couldn't figure out, Marshall's father was there playing grandfather. He hadn't asked why Cary's own father hadn't come down, though he knew their relationship had been rocky at best since Cary's mother had died.

"Get over yourself," he told himself as he stared at himself in the rearview. He was nervous. He'd fallen for Cary, even though he still couldn't give either of them all that they needed. He was gone over Gus from the moment the sick boy had asked for him a couple weeks ago. He was scared shitless over what that meant but he knew he wouldn't let them down by not going to this party.

So he grabbed up his beer and the gift, took a deep breath and headed up the driveway. When he knocked on the door, he hoped like hell it'd be Cary who answered. No such luck. A leather-tanned old man with gray-blond hair and dull blue eyes was there when the door swung open.

"Ah, you must be the fella," the old guy said, divesting Heath of the gift tucked under his arm. "Manny Keller, son, nice to meet you. The insanity is in there so this is your last chance to back out." Heath laughed and took the man's proffered hand.

"I s'pose I came expecting it so I'm here to assist."

"Nonsense," Manny said. "Celine and Cary are handling everything. Won't even let me stack gifts. May as well come in and grab a beer."

Heath followed him in and immediately was overwhelmed with the noise. There were a few kids running around with Gus and what appeared to be two or three parents gathered around talking to Cary. Cary looked flustered but happy when his eyes lit on Heath. He made excuses and came over. He leaned up as if to kiss Heath, but apparently thought better of it, touching Heath's forearm instead, looking toward the watchful mothers in the kitchen. They were all making that face that women like to make when something is cute, so apparently they were dealing with a friendly crowd.

Not that Heath gave two shits either way. He wrapped a hand around Cary's neck and kissed him, nibbling on his bottom lip, but stopping just at the line before getting racy in front of a bunch of four year olds.

Cary's face was flushed when Heath ended the kiss and Heath felt a surge of pride at having that effect on the man.

"Thanks for coming," Cary said, breathless.

"Wouldn't miss it." And he meant it. He was glad he'd gotten over it and come in. He made the rounds with Cary, getting a double cheeked kiss from Celine, shaking hands with Kent and getting introduced to the moms whose children, he found out, went to pre-school with Gus. Cary stumbled over what to say when he introduced Heath, frowning and glancing at Heath. Heath felt it was well worth the smile he got in return when he introduced himself. "I'm the boyfriend. Heath Cummings. Nice to meet you."

Cary squeezed Heath's hand before running off to stop something or other from getting broken. Heath went to grab a beer to settle his nerves. While he was quite out to his family and personal friends, at his local bar, he'd not been this open—never really had a reason to be before. He was slightly anxious, which he knew was ridiculous. None of the mothers mentioned their husbands also working the rigs and it was highly unlikely any of his coworkers would show up at this particular birthday party. That's why he'd enjoyed working for his company in particular. Most of the guys were from Mobile or random dots on the map in Texas. He could only think of one coworker in the area and he was not the type to befriend dog bakery owning gay men.

"You alright over here, son?" Manny asked. He'd appeared out of seemingly nowhere, though it wouldn't be too hard to sneak up on anyone as loud as it was in there.

"Yessir. Just trying to stay out of the way."

"I hear from Miss Celine you've been taking good care of my boys."

Heath dipped his head. "I try, but I'm new at all this."

Manny patted Heath on his arm, grandfatherly and kind. "You're doing fine. I've not seen them so spirited since... well, in a very, very long time. Especially our Cary. So new at this or not, you're apparently doing something right."

"I'm glad," Heath said, probably too quietly to hear over the racket. Manny gave him a firm pat on the back and wandered back off to the recliner.

The whole thing felt like a blur of cake and squeals and ripped wrapping paper. Cary had only seen anything similar at his nephew's birthday parties, but his brother was too rigid to have a bunch of screaming kids in his house so it'd been a much quieter affair with one or two well-behaved kids from their church. This was louder, but he could see where this was a better party by a mile. Gus looked like a kid for once, rather than the strangely thoughtful old man who sat staring at pictures in his books—or getting filthy.

"This one's from Heath," Cary said. He was holding Gus in his lap as the boy ripped into his gifts, making sure Gus thanked each person.

"Heaf!" Gus said, snatching the gift. He tore into it and Heath hoped it wasn't a completely ridiculous gift. Cary laughed out loud as Gus let out an "Oh, wow!" and pulled out the sailor's uniform and the plastic boat. Now that Heath looked at it, the uniform looked awfully big for the little boy and the boat was probably a toy suited for a much older child.

"Sorry it's so big. I told the sales clerk lady he was four and—" he held out his hands "—this big. She said that size should work." He blushed, he couldn't help it when all the moms gave him the 'you poor, bumbling idiot' look.

"It's perfect," Cary said. Gus didn't just thank him like he did the rest, though. He jumped from Cary's lap and ran over to hug Heath's leg. Heath may have had dust in his eye for a second there.

When Gus ran back over to finish with his presents Celine nudged him with her shoulder. She was smiling at him. "Well done."

He sighed. "I tried. For my nephew they wanted socks and sweaters, no toys. But I saw the boat and... Yeah. It's just so big. A 4T, she said."

"Ah, yes. But this is good. He's small now, but he'll grow into it."

"So it wasn't the right size?"

"Our Gus was a preemie, so he's always been small." Huh, that was news. "He's still a 2T. But parents always love to get larger clothes. Maybe by Halloween he will be able to wear it, no?"

He nodded, not taking his eyes off Cary and Gus.

"He did not tell you Gus was premature?" she asked. He shook his head. "Ah, yes. Only a month early but enough to be worrisome. He was very small. But Cary would have none of our sympathy. He just did it. Sat with that baby until he was out of the NICU. This is why he did not say anything, I'm sure. It was such a non-issue for him. This was his son. He did what he had to do, you understand?"

Heath did understand, and he smiled at Celine to let her know. He just couldn't get over it, though. No wonder the Whitmore boys had barreled into his life and bowled him over. He never had a choice. They were fighters, they were strong and beautiful and he hadn't realized until that moment how lucky he was that Gus was alive, how lucky he was Cary had given him a chance, and what a gift Cary had given in sharing his little blessing. And didn't it beat all that he considered a child a blessing. He hadn't thought that about his own.

"*Sometimes things just work out how they're supposed to.*"

Heath kept his eyes on Cary, watching as they finished presents, and Cary slipped into the kitchen to pour himself some tea. Heath slipped in behind him and Cary started when he turned around. "Hey, you, you surprised me. Having an okay time? Sorry it's so crazy but it shouldn't last much longer."

"You're amazing, you know that." Statement, not a question. Cary's eyes held a question as his face flushed. Heath bent his head and kissed Cary firmly, placing a hand over Cary's heart. God, but this man was something he didn't even know he'd wanted, yet here he was, kissing him, changing his whole fucking life.

Now Heath just had to figure out how to keep it. And fuck knows he wanted that more than anything. But could he change everything about his life after just four months? He didn't know the answer to that, but looking at the contented look on Cary's face as he place his head on Heath's chest and hugged him tight, he didn't think he had much of a choice.

Chapter 11

Cary was not having a good week. Inventory had been off, he wasn't sure how, but that wasn't enough to really hurt profits. What had been the kick in the teeth had been when the refrigerator had given out the night before while they'd been closed, so not only had he been out fresh ingredients, lost business during the day because they were missing favorite menu items, and had to replace the fresh items; he'd had to buy a new refrigerator.

Thankfully, they'd had a little money in reserve to help with those things, but it was still enough of a hit to make Cary flinch when he crunched the numbers and saw how badly they'd done for the week, financially. Then Gus had gotten sick again and had to be rushed to the emergency room and there'd been no one to help with the shop, so he'd had to close for the day.

Now he was playing catch up, running around like he'd lost his head. And he hadn't seen Heath in almost three weeks. Heath and his team had a class they had to take in Houston for the company, so he was losing a few days of off time. Then Heath's parents had called him to come help with a repair project on their house. Heath's dad had had a stroke a few years back and needed help with heavy work around home, so Heath volunteered to fly there, promising he'd spend the weekend with Cary when he got back.

Of course Cary understood. He wasn't a jerk, and he knew Heath loved his parents. Cary wouldn't call his dad if his house was on fire, but they'd been estranged for so long that thinking about it didn't even bother him anymore. Cary just missed his boyfriend. Missed his smell and his laugh and waking up with him. He was well and truly in love with the man. Five little months and he wasn't sure how he'd ever deal if Heath were to leave his and Gus's lives.

But Heath was more and more affectionate, loving. They still hadn't said the words, but Cary felt it in his bones, they were solid. He hoped. He was getting a little antsy, wanting to say the words, wanting to hear them back. But he was trying not to push. Heath had made such strides from childless bachelor to boyfriend who made an effort to be involved. And five months really wasn't all that long was it?

No. No, he wouldn't sweat it. He'd let go of the

reigns and let it happen. They were good. Things were awesome. Heath had only six or so more months before he could quit the off-shore job, then the pressure would be off, the closet door all the way open. Cary could give the man a few more months.

But fuck... Could this week get any worse? He could at least use a hug from Heath instead of a few text messages a day.

"Hey, Cary. I, uh, think you should come handle this," Kent said, peeking his head in the office.

Cary groaned. "Please don't let it be more bad news."

Kent's expression didn't give Cary much confidence. He shoved back from his desk and walked out into the store front. *This is what you get for asking if things can get worse.*

There, with his news reporter hair and chiseled jaw, stood Marshall freakin' Keller, dressed to the nines. "M-Marshall?" Cary stuttered, not sure what to think.

"That's who I was afraid it was," Kent mumbled behind Cary.

"What are you doing here?" Cary asked, scowling.

Marshall had the grace to look contrite. "Sorry

to bother you at work. But I'm not in town long and... I really wanted to talk to you."

"What for? I can't imagine there's much to say?" *Why now? Why this week?*

"I won't beg, but I'd appreciate if you'd hear me out."

Cary turned to Kent and held his breath, counting silently.

"I can get rid of him," Kent said.

Cary shook his head. "No, I'll deal with it. Don't want him popping up every time he comes to town." Kent gave a curt nod after looking at Cary like he was insane. Yeah, he probably was. Part of him wanted to know what Marshall had to say. Oh, he was well and truly over the man, but the righteously indignant part of him wanted to know what the jerk wanted.

"Follow me," Cary said over his shoulder, going into the back. No way would he lock them in the small office. The office was full of him and Heath, their first time. No, if Marshall wanted to sit, he could sit on the stacked bags of dry dog food.

When Marshall finally came in, he looked around. "You've done great things with the place. One of the vets I know said she recommends your stuff to her clients all the time."

"Really? You want to make small talk?"

Marshall bowed his head, putting his hands in his pocket. "No." He looked up, not quite meeting Cary's eyes. "I just... You look good, Care."

"Thanks," Cary snapped, crossing his arms over his chest.

"My dad tells me Gus is four now. That's crazy."

"Still with the small talk?"

Marshall winced at Cary's tone. "Sorry, just. I like the name. Gus. Very you."

"Very Gus. He's... he's great. No thanks to you," Cary said petulantly. Didn't he just sound like a high schooler. He'd imagined this scenario a million times and this is not how he'd pictured it going. "Again... please... get to the point, Marshall. It's been a long week."

"I just wanted to check on you, I guess. I know I have no right, but my dad with the old Jewish guilt keeps me up to date, so I can have my asshole behavior rubbed in my face once a month."

"Do you want me to apologize for him?"

"No. I deserve it." He clasped his hands together. "He tells me you've found someone that treats you and Gus well, and I guess I felt jealous when I heard it and since I was in town... I had to see for myself how badly I fucked up."

Cary threw his hands up. "Seriously? This is what? Some kind of self-flagellation?"

Marshall closed his eyes and sighed. "Yeah. You could call it that. And I guess I thought you deserved to really cuss me out."

"I try not to cuss. Little ears."

"Not gonna give me the satisfaction, huh?" Marshal asked with a wry grin. "Some things never change. I have missed you. And I am sorry. I know my reasons were horrible, but I'm glad you've been happy. If you need anything..."

"We don't."

"Fair enough." Marshall edged toward the door.

"So... that's it?" Cary was a little flabbergasted.

"I didn't come to disrupt your life. I just thought you deserved that apology. I appreciate you letting my dad have contact with your son."

"He didn't leave, Marshall." Marshall's shoulders rounded. Without another word, he was gone, leaving Cary to gape at the door. Had that really just happened?

"You okay, boss?" Kent said, coming into the back.

"I'm... Wow."

"That didn't last long."

"Just long enough to make my blood pressure go through the roof," Cary snarled. "That was the strangest thing I've ever experienced."

"Do you need to head out?"

Cary went into the office and kicked his rolling chair for good measure before slumping into it. Kent behind him. "No. I'll be fine. I need to keep my mind off this terrible week. Which he *would* show up this week, right? Like I needed more to deal with."

"Don't they always appear when you need them least," Kent said, patting Cary's shoulder. "If I can do anything, let me know."

Cary pulled a Heath and grunted before turning back to his computer. Marshall Keller. Who'd have imagined that twist to his week? He realized he was gnashing his teeth. He wasn't angry for himself. He was angry for Gus. Though, he shouldn't be. Gus had plenty of people in his life to love and care for him. But Marshall had abandoned Gus and that was beyond unforgivable.

Cary leaned back in his chair and ran his fingers through his hair. Heath, he needed to see Heath. He needed a hug from Gus, too. He needed his guys. He pulled out his phone to see if he had any new messages and sure enough *Heath*.

Be home tonight. Come out if you can get away, if not I'll come there tmo.

Cary smiled. Finally, a bright spot. One more crappy thing this week and he was seriously gonna yank his hair out in chunks.

Great. See you tonight. He replied.

He could run home, beg Celine, give Gus love and go get a few minutes with his guy, even if he couldn't stay the night it'd be worth it just for a few minutes to catch his breath, and maybe an orgasm.

Chapter 12

Heath was fucking exhausted. It had been a crazy week, and worse, he knew Cary's week had been shit. He was so happy to be home. Driving the twenty minutes from the airport seemed to be taking longer than any other leg of the journey. He could already smell his own sheets, feel Cary wrapping around him.

Before the unscheduled trip to his parents' house, it'd been work and classes, constant ragging from the guys who'd overheard him saying goodbye to a Cary so they figured out he was seeing someone, though they figured it was a girl. He supposed at least with that assumption he didn't have to pussyfoot. He didn't know why he hadn't thought of it yet, but no one would accuse him of being smart. Though, allowing them to assume Cary was a girl smarted, knowing Cary would probably be hurt by it. Cary had been more understanding about Heath being in the closet than other guys he'd fooled around with.

Cary was just... Cary. Heath still couldn't believe he'd gotten so lucky, knew he didn't deserve it. He was almost there, though. If Cary could just hold out a little longer, he'd be able to be out and not worry about becoming fucking shark bait.

When he pulled in the marina's parking lot he noticed a couple of pickups with people sitting on the tailgates. They appeared to be drinking. It wouldn't be the first time Heath'd had to run off local kids who thought once it was dark the parking lot would be deserted. He was technically the only person who *lived* there but that still didn't mean a bunch of kids should hang out, breaking bottles and fucking up the —

"Oh, fuck," he said, smacking his steering wheel. He pulled in the lot beside the trucks.

"Woo! It's Cummings!" was followed by a chorus of "Cummings!" *Fuck, fuck, fuck!*

"Guys," he said. "What are you doin' here?" *Seriously, what the fuck?*

"We told you we were coming," one of the welders on his team, Roy, said. There were four of them and... even better, they'd brought dates.

"I don't remember hearing that."

"Hell, yeah," said another driller, John. "We said we'd come down to celebrate bein' done with that damn class." Then they all cheered and clinked their beer bottles together. He remembered a conversation similar to that but he didn't realize...

"So here were are." John said, throwing an arm around Heath's shoulder. The bastard smelled like beer was leaking from his pores. Oh wait, that was the beer he was spilling on Heath's shirt. Heath ducked out from under the man's arm.

"I didn't know y'all meant my boat. I can't sleep this many people," he said, wiping the beer off himself best as he could. He pulled his duffel from the back of his Jeep.

"Sure you can," a female voice piped up. Heath closed his eyes, realizing just how much trouble he was about to be in. That voice was Chastity—Charity? Christy! He looked at her and she smiled, lashes fluttering. "You got room for eight, especially if we double up."

"Ain't gonna happen," he said, leaving no room for argument. "How drunk are y'all?"

"We been here three hours waitin' for your sorry ass," Roy said. They were all pretty wasted.

"Y'all aren't staying, but you can hang out until I can get a designated driver out here. We'll get y'all settled at the Motel 6 over in Navarre. It's cheap and beach front."

That was met with an unhappy chorus of groans

and curse words. *Fuck.* He immediately pulled out his phone, dialing Cary. It rang several times but went to voicemail. *Must still be at work.*

He dialed Kyle who picked up after a few rings. "Yo?"

"I have a drunk crew from my rig who decided to drop in for the fucking weekend and Cary on his way. I need them gone, like now."

"Shiiiit," Kyle said, drawing it out. Heath heard a few thunks and bangs. "Okay. On it. Should be there in about fifteen. Maybe I can take 'em to my boat? Think that'll keep 'em happy?"

"Whatever you gotta do. They just can't be on mine."

"On my way." They disconnected and Heath boarded the *Keep Swimming*. He hoped like hell the drunk brigade would stay ashore, but of course that hope burst as the yacht rocked with all of them hopping on the deck.

"Okay, guys. My buddy is on his way to take you over to his boat where you won't be bothering me."

That seemed to please them more than the motel idea, all of them whooping noisily. Good thing he didn't have neighbors, otherwise he may be evicted. This was fucked. And if Cary showed up while they were here, there had to be a way to keep the bullshit to a minimum. They were drunk anyway, so they'd probably not even notice if he slipped Cary inside and explained the fuck up to him.

He tried calling Cary's cell once more while he went down to his room to drop his duffel. "C'mon, answer..."

"You've reached Cary—" He punched the end button.

"Fuck!" He threw his phone down, yanking the beer soaked t-shirt over his head and going into the bathroom to wash the smell off his hands and shoulder. He stomped back in his room, cursing the universe and the ugly damn stars, hoping Kyle would hurry his ass up. He heard banging around in the galley and realized the guys were now raiding his beer. *Fucking great. Just great.* Just what he needed, for them to get trashed and pass out all over the place. Five more minutes and he was just gonna kick their asses out.

He went to his dresser and yanked open drawers, finding no clean shirts. Everything in his duffel was dirty, too, waiting to go over to Cary's for laundry day. He had an *aha!* moment and went for Cary's drawer. He pulled out the large black 13 Bar t-shirt Cary sometimes slept in. When he turned back to his room, fuck. Fuck. There was Christy.

"Long time no see, Heathy." *Oh, she's the Heathy one.*

"Yeah, what's up? Y'all need something out there?"

"No, your boys are good. I just thought I'd come check on you. Been a while," she purred. She placed a hand on his chest, and God help him, but his body responded, of course it responded. He liked women, he had *had* this particular woman. For all her purring and words like *Heathy* he remembered her body. Hell, he hadn't had sex in three weeks and he was so wound up with wantin' Cary, the wind coulda done it for him right now, but dammit, he didn't want her body and he felt guilty for even getting hard.

"Christy, I can't. I'm seeing someone, okay?"

"Don't be a pussy!" One of the guys called into the room. Christy laughed low in her throat, casting her eyes down at his hard-on.

"Doesn't look like your body wants to say no." Her hand started moving down his chest, to his stomach. He didn't want this. He wanted Cary, his body, his arms around him. Yeah, he liked women but he *loved* Cary. His body may say yes to fucking a potato, but he wouldn't do this to Cary. He had to think of a way to get out of this situation. Seemed the 'seeing someone' thing was working for the roughneck groupie. Of course, that was his rude ass cock's fault. She had enough booze in her—he could smell it on her breath—that only a flat out *fuck off* was going to work. *Please don't let her make a damn scene. And what do I do if she does?*

"Look, —"

"What in the hell?" Heath felt all the color bleed from his face. Christy frowned and looked toward the door.

"Oh, hey, it's kennel boy. You have a cute kid," she slurred a little. Cary's eyes were wide with shock, chin trembling.

"Ca—" Fuck. He couldn't say his name. They guys.

"Sorry kennel boy, we're a little busy," Christy purred. "Unless you want to join?" Cary's eyes flicked down to Heath's hard-on, which had flagged considerably, but not enough to be missed. Damn thing. A tear slid down Cary's cheek and he stormed out.

"Fuck!" Heath bellowed, shoving away. He followed, waving the guys off when they tried to ask him what his friend's deal was. Christy called after him, but he *had* to get to Cary. He'd blocked out any possible repercussions with his co-workers, he had to get there before Cary left.

He made it just as Cary was unlocking his car. "Cary, stop!"

When Cary looked up, Heath's heart stopped. His cheeks were tracked with tears, he looked utterly distraught. "What, Heath? What could you possibly want?"

"Cary, just listen."

"Shouldn't you get back to Christy?"

"Cary, I tried to call you and warn you. Kyle is on his way to get them. And nothing fucking happened!"

"Because I walked in. You looked like you were having a pretty *hard* time." Cary wasn't crying out of despair any more, but out of sheer anger.

"Cary, no. I was about to tell her to fuck off. I just had to do it without gettin' her wound up and—"

"Outing you? What would you have done if she *had* gotten wound up?"

Heath paused, he'd wondered that himself, but he knew he wouldn't have done anything. He wouldn't. "Cary."

Apparently the pause before his answer had

been a mistake because Cary threw his hands up. "No. See, this... you can have sex women. I get that. I accept that. You *like* being with them, so would it be torture to do it if it meant keeping those guys off your back?"

"Yes! I wouldn't do that to you!"

Cary shook his head, scoffing. "Even if you didn't plan on doing anything, how far would you go to stay in your closet? Where's your line? I'm okay with your closet, I just didn't realize being in it made you untrustworthy."

"That's not fair." Heath was freaking out. He didn't know what to say.

"No, what's not fair was me having to walk in on that." Heath opened his mouth to speak but he heard his name being called and looked back to see one of the guys calling him back.

Cary leveled Heath with his gaze. "Well, you've got a party to attend. And don't worry, your closet door's closed tight. Go have fun with Christy."

"Cary, just give me twenty minutes. Kyle is getting them out of here and I'll come over."

"Fuck. You." Cary snapped. Heath reeled back. His Cary didn't talk to people like that. His Cary never cussed beyond the occasional *hell* or *damn* unless they were in the middle of having sex. Heath's heart dropped at the harsh words being directed at him.

"Cary?"

Cary hopped in his car, cranked it and backed away. So many things had happened in the last fifteen goddamn minutes he didn't know which to respond to first. The only thing he knew was he'd fucked up. Again. And he didn't think dirt clodded daisies would fix it this time.

He stood there, watching as Cary's tail-lights disappeared, and a minute after, until Christy walked up behind him and wrapped nimble fingers around his bicep. "What's your friend's problem?"

He glared at her, jerking his arm from her grip. She looked stunned, but headlights blinding them stopped either of them from saying anything. A familiar SUV pulled up beside them and Kyle stuck his head out. "Drunk Express at your service." He frowned when he recognized Christy and flicked his eyes up at Heath. "Please tell me I made it before Cary."

Heath's shoulders slumped and he choked on any words he had. He shook his head and when Christy touched him again he looked at her and fucking *roared* in her face. She took several steps back, eyes wide. "Get. The fuck. Off of me!" he bit out.

"Oh, fuck," Kyle said. He bound from the SVU

and followed silently behind Heath.

As he climbed aboard he couldn't see any more. His vision was blurry for some goddamned reason. It wasn't like seeing red, or even like being angry. His chest hurt so bad. He started pounding it, trying to stop the ache. When one of the guys tried to ask him a question, he snatched the bottle out of the man's hand and slung it across the room. Then he did it to the next guy.

"Out! Get the fuck out!" he bellowed. "Now!"

He went to his room and banged against the closet door, then hit his chest again, trying to get that damn fucking piece of shit aching to stop.

"Hey, buddy. Hey, hey, hey..." Kyle's voice was soothing and when Heath turned to him, he had his hands in front of him, motioning for him to bring it down a notch.

"What the fuck?!" His yell was hoarse, then he plopped to sitting on the bed and dug his fingers in his chest. Why wouldn't it *stop hurting*?

Kyle shut the door behind himself and took a knee in front of Heath. "Hey, Heath, buddy. You're okay. You're good."

"It hurts. I think it's a panic attack or something." He smacked his chest again, but Kyle grabbed his hand and stilled it. Then with his other hand he reached up and wiped Heath's cheek. When he pulled the hand away and it was wet he dried it on his pants leg.

"Did Cary see something?" Kyle asked quietly.

"I couldn't think of how to get her to stop without outing myself. I was gonna tell her to get her drunk ass off me, but Cary came in and he's so mad. I was hard... I mean... it was just a reaction but I'd never..."

Kyle grimaced sympathetically. "Cary break things off?"

"I think so," he said miserably. Fuck, his chest hurt again, like he was empty in there and it was trying to cave in. He tried to bang on it again, but Kyle held his hand firmly and wiped Heath's wet cheeks again.

"Big guy, that's your heart breaking."

"I didn't know it hurt physically." That wasn't possible. Why did people write songs about this shit if it felt like hell? Who wanted to relive *this* over and over?

Kyle smiled gently. "There's a lot about that particular organ you didn't know until recently. I hate you had to find out the hard way."

"Make it stop," Heath pleaded.

Kyle sighed and shook his head sadly. "Nothing I can do." There was a banging up on deck. "Shit. Look, Heath, I gotta make sure your crew gets somewhere. They're so drunk I doubt they'll know what's going on. I'll cover your ass with them. Best thing you can do is get a shower and get into bed. We'll have to deal with this one thing at a time."

Heath nodded, lamely. Kyle wrapped his arms around him and Heath couldn't stop himself from clinging for a moment. This is not how it was supposed to go down. He'd tried to get her off him. He tried to do the right thing. How had this happened?

"Shower then sleep. I'll be here when you wake up," Kyle said. Then he was gone. Heath fell back on the bed and closed his eyes tight, pleading for this to be a really bad dream, or some drunken hallucination. But then that vacuum feeling started in his chest again and all he could do was curl up at the foot of the bed and wait. Wait for it to stop feeling like that, wait to stop feeling anything at all. He'd been fine when he didn't feel anything. Nothing wasn't worth *this*. Was it?

Then he saw Cary's face smiling, and Gus and Cary on the beach with him and goddammit. He cried. For the first time since he was probably ten years old Heath cried like a fucking baby.

Chapter 13

"Good morning, beautiful," Celine said, voice wandering through the funk and the fuzz that was Cary waking up feeling like garbage. He groaned and rolled over, covering his head with the throw pillow. His head was killing him. Rolling over made his stomach lurch and that made him even more annoyed that he was awake in the first place.

"Sit up, now. I have café," she coaxed, using her gentlest, most maternal tones.

"What time is it?"

"It's early yet. The tiny human is still sleeping, but I have to go to work and I wanted to check on you first. Now, up you get." She patted his back gently.

He groaned again but rolled to sitting, throwing his legs over the side of the couch, where he'd slept the night before, fully dressed. He took the mug of coffee from her and sipped. *Yes!* So good. His stomach protested feebly but he needed the caffeine if she was waking him at six a.m.

"How are you feeling?"

"Horrible." Wasn't that an understatement? But the most all encompassing word for how he felt in general. His head was pounding, eyes were gritty, heart aching, and stomach nauseous. Very nauseous.

"This is what you get for drinking yourself to sleep."

Cary scrunched his face up and rolled his eyes unhappily at the mention of drinking. "I didn't drink." Her responding snort was disbelieving. "I didn't," he said fervently. "Honestly. But I did eat two pints of that stupid gelato you left over here."

Celine sniffed delicately. "I would have preferred you'd drunk all my wine. That gelato is harder to find you silly goose."

"Me too," Cary replied. "I'm pretty sure the sugar hangover is worse than a wine hangover. And at least I would have gotten more than an hour of sleep."

Celine's cold—her bony fingers were chronically chilly— gentle hand touched Cary's head, stroking back his undoubtedly wild bed head, nearly making Cary's stupid waterworks start up again. Then he realized with some oddly clinical distance from himself that there really wasn't anything left in the well to pour out.

"Your face is doing strange things."

He huffed an mirthless laugh. "I was actually

just realizing I didn't have any more crying to do."

"Well, this is good, no?"

"I suppose." Cary gave her a strained smile, her compassionate gaze driving him crazy. "Hey, this is not the worst ever. And you warned me to be careful right?"

"To say I'm not a bit surprised would be a lie. I thought maybe I'd been wrong, though. You seemed so nice together."

"Well, sometimes things just don't work. Perhaps I'm just too insecure to be with a closet case."

"I'm just so very sorry." Cary felt silly being comforted by this woman who'd lost the love of her life, an American photographer who was killed in South America while assisting with filming a documentary. His and Heath's breakup, one that seemed inevitable, was trivial compared to Celine's loss. It seemed trivial compared to many things they'd both been through over the years.

"No sense losing my mind over it, right?" he asked. She seemed concerned as soon as the words left his mouth. "Really, I'll be fine. At the end of the day I have to move on. I've got Gus and The Barkery and this was six months with someone who..." He couldn't remember what he'd wanted to say, and he let his thought trail off.

"You loved. Someone you loved."

Cary flicked a startled gaze her way. She laughed and patted his head like a puppy. "You're rather transparent, my friend. Can I ask a question?" Cary eyed her warily but nodded. "Could you have misunderstood the situation?"

Cary pinched the bridge of his nose. "At first, that's what I thought I'd done. I just flipped out. But what else was I supposed to think? Her hand was right above his belt and he was..." He cleared his throat, a little embarrassed to be reliving the night.

"Hard?"

"Yes. God." He jumped to standing and paced a couple times before she held out her hand. He sighed and took it, sitting back down beside her. "I was so pissed. Then I was even more pissed because I couldn't out him to his crew. I couldn't fight with him there. Then he followed me and when I asked how far he'd go..." That'd been the worst part. He'd wanted so badly to think this was just another one of Heath's stumbles, one of those moments where one of them had just done something dumb that they could talk out. "He paused, Celine. He fucking paused. He didn't know any more than I did how far he would have gone if it'd come down to fucking her to stay in the closet or outing himself in front of all those guys."

"Sounds like a difficult situation. For both of you. I, like you, do not think I would be able to forgive so easily. But maybe you should talk now you've had time to think more clearly?"

"No," he said, sadly. "This is just too much, you know? And he's still got months to go before he can be out. I *do* understand his reasons. Being closeted was never the issue. But now, can I trust him? And really? When is enough enough? If it wasn't one thing it was another. He freaked out because he liked me, didn't call for a week; then any time I go to his yacht I risk getting surprised by someone he's fucked, this time one of them pawing him and his hard-on."

Celine furrowed her brow, patted his knee. "I cannot answer that. I understand, though. You have been burned badly once before. And that is... an untenable?" Cary laughed and confirmed the word would be appropriate. "An untenable situation. But do not forget the good times. Even if you do end this for good, remember how much he did care for you. Those will be better memories to have in your heart in the future. He reminded you that you *can* love again, even after Marshall and the heartache he left you with."

"You're right." He lay his head on her shoulder.

"He's a good guy. He was good to Gus, and that... that means the world."

"So what do you wish to do now?" she asked as she lay her cheek on top of his head.

"Just... I want to get back to work. I've wallowed enough for one day. I just want to not think about it for a while. It's permanently etched in my damn brain, seeing her touching him. I need to distract myself from that image"

"And what would make you reconsider and forgive him?"

Cary leaned back on the couch and stared at the ceiling, counting the beams that criss-crossed there. What would make him reconsider? Could he? "I honestly can't say. I get... I get that I need to work on how insecure I have been from the beginning about him being with women. I've always kind of known that was an irrational insecurity. Maybe some of me blowing up was this horrible week I had and confronting Marshall yesterday. But his pause, his being unsure of himself... Maybe if he came back after he's completely out? But I don't know if even then it'd be too little, too late."

"Ah, it is never too late for love, chéri. But I understand by then this love may be water under the bridge. Maybe it has run its natural course, as they say."

"Yeah," he sighed. Run its course. Sounded about right. Getting involved with someone who'd said himself that he was a bad bet should have told him the course would have been a short one to run.

"Anyway," he said, sitting up on the couch and downing the last of his coffee. He gave her a more genuine smile and bussed a kiss on her cheek as he stood. "I have got to get moving. I gotta get Gus ready and get to work in a few hours."

She stood and hugged him tight. And here came those waterworks from that well he thought he'd cried dry. Crap. "Take care of yourself, Cary." She pulled back and held him at arm's length. "You are a good man, as is he—even if you both are lost in your own ways. You will figure this out, one way or another." They said fond farewells as he walked her out. She was right. Either way, he'd be okay. Today he could be sad, maybe even cry some more, but he would be okay.

****

"You talk to him. He's too busy pouting like a bitch for me to do any good," Kyle said into his cell phone before tossing it next to Heath where he was still lying on his bed. He'd gotten up a few times, but always seemed to find himself back there. His chest didn't hurt so much anymore, but that wasn't necessarily good because now he was numb and he hated that almost as much as he hated the pain. He couldn't believe he had wished he would stop feeling anything at all. This sucked.

"Pick up the phone, Heath," Kyle said impatiently. Heath glared, but Kyle could play that game too and Heath just didn't have the energy to keep at it.

He picked the phone and checked the screen to see who he'd be talking to. *Shit.* "Really, you sicced Becca on me?" He glowered at his best friend, who just shrugged and mumbled about desperate times.

"I heard that," Becca sniped loud enough for Heath to hear through the ear piece.

He put the phone to his ear. "I had no doubt. That was kinda the point."

"Shut up, Heath. I did not take time out of my Friday with *my* boyfriend—which I'm getting dirty looks over, thanks for that—for you to not listen to me."

"I thought that was one of the big no-nos."

"It is, obviously. Which is why I'm only going to be on here for thirty seconds. I've never held your hand before and I'm not gonna do it now. What you're gonna do now is get out of that fucking bed, get it together, and listen to Kyle. The end."

"Why would I listen to him?" Heath teased, not knowing where his ability to tease was even coming from, him being in such a black mood.

"Because he's better at this stuff than either you or me, and you'd know that if you ever listened to him. That's why I'm saying listen to him," she said kindly.

"Do *you*?"

"More than you know."

"When did my exes start a club?"

"Well, there're enough of us cast-offs to start an alumni association, Heath."

"I hate you," he grumbled.

"Of course you do. Now I'm going to get laid. Goodbye." With that, she disconnected. He was smiling now, though, so she'd obviously accomplished something. Kyle walked back in just in time to see Heath upright, having pushed himself to sitting.

"Oh, good. She got you to move. That's something, I guess." Kyle tossed Heath a beer and bounced as he landed on the bed next to Heath with his own beer in hand. "So, buddy, I have to begin with, you're a dumbass."

"Thanks," Heath drawled, popping the top off his beer and drinking.

"But we've been through that, so I'll ask next, why in the hell did you let them come on the damn yacht?"

"Because I'm a dumbass?"

"Good answer, but I'm looking for a better explanation that that," Kyle said, shoving Heath over so he could lean back against the headboard next to him.

"They were drunk and fucking shit up in the parking lot. I figured you'd get here soon and it couldn't hurt. Better than them getting arrested. They're my crew, you know."

"Why didn't you warn Cary?"

"I tried to call him twice but it rang and rang." Heath knew in hindsight a voicemail would have been smart. "I was so tired from traveling, and everything was just nuts. I was freaking out."

"And the girl? You hooked up with her before, right?"

"I think that's what made it worse. Maybe if it'd been someone random, but he recognized her before he even saw I had a hard-on. But Kyle, I really wasn't going to do anything with Christy. I was shaken, didn't know how to handle it, but I would never."

"I know," Kyle said sincerely. "I think Cary knows that, too. But... okay, let me say; A: no one wants to be embarrassed like that in front of tons of people, especially when they want to queen the fuck out but have enough restrain not to out someone, namely you, B: no gay man wants to be left for or cheated on with a woman, it's just a fact, and C: nothing drives a gay man as bat shit crazy as dating a closet case. The pause, that's what killed you."

Heath chugged his beer, finishing the bottle off. "You think I don't know that? All of that?"

"You guys have had a few bumps in the road, more than once, over those same issues. Maybe it just wasn't meant to be?"

"Huh," Heath grunted. Kyle chuckled and patted his shoulder before getting off the bed. He left the room and came back with another couple beers.

When they'd settled back with freshly opened bottles, Heath had to ask, "What do I do?"

"I don't know there's anything to do."

"How can that be?"

"Heath, man, you can't make him not be weird

about this stuff. He's been super understanding about the closet issue, but he's been surrounded by your ex-fucks. I don't get the weirdness, I'm just not jealous like that, but I think that's something he'd need to work out for himself. And so long as you're in the closet and your buddies are bringing around roughneck groupies you've used hard and put up wet, he's going to have a hard time."

Heath snarled. "What the fuck do I do about that, though? I have bills to pay. I'm close, but not close enough, to being able to quit the roughnecking."

Kyle grimaced. "Yeah, and we didn't get the Conklin contract so it's not the best time for you to quit if you insist on not bringing in business partners." They'd had that disagreement several times. He was close enough to paying off his second investment, the *Keep Swimming*, and he'd bought Kyle's boat free and clear. He didn't want to be beholden to anyone. This was his dream and he could do it on his own.

"This is why I didn't date, you know. Before, I didn't answer to anyone, I didn't have to worry about shit. I just worked, paid off my boat, fucked who I wanted, and got to live the dream."

"Yes," Kyle said. "Very mature of you."

Heath glanced at his friend. "What makes you

the authority on maturity?"

"Well, I know I wouldn't give up someone I love because I want to hold on to the same priorities I've had since I was fifteen."

"What the fuck does that mean?" Heath snapped.

"Heath, for fuck's sake!" Kyle sat up and looked Heath in the eye. "You are the bachelor type. I get it. Your priorities are 'Heath, the *Keep Swimming*, and Heath.' There's nothing wrong with that."

Heath reeled back. "Is that what you really think?"

Kyle looked at Heath like he was the dumbest person he'd ever seen. "That's not what I *think*. That's what you've said. I just quoted *you*, verbatim."

Heath blinked, then looked down, eyes wide as he stared without focus and peeled at the label on his beer. Had he really said that?

"Heath, there's nothing wrong with that. You're not a jerk. You help anyone out when they need it. When I finished school you gave me this job. You just aren't cut out to focus all of your energy on another person. That's why you've not dated, that's why you didn't want kids. There's absolutely nothing wrong with it. Better to be honest than bring some kid into the world you can't be there for. That's why so many kids are fucked up these days."

Heath looked up, vision blurry—dammit—and let out a shaky breath. "But I want more than that. I want Cary. And Gus. I want to matter to them." Holy shit. When had that happened? When had he not realized they were important to him and he wanted to be just as important to them. When had he been blindsided by those two?

He knew, though. It'd been that first trip on the boat. He remembered the fleeting thought that he would sell all his worldly possessions if it meant a lifetime of days like that one day. He hadn't been looking for it, didn't need to be fixed or changed, didn't require a family or love to survive. But now he'd had it and he wanted to keep it. He fucking wanted it and he wanted it with Cary and Gus Whitmore.

Kyle said Heath's name and he realized it must not have been the first time. "What are you thinking, buddy?" Kyle asked.

"I'm thinking..." Another shaky breath. "I fucked up." A tear slid down his cheek. That could stop any time now, so far as Heath was concerned.

"Well, only way to un-fuck it, assuming it's not too late, is priorities, my man."

"But how do you give up on everything you've wanted for so long?"

"First, you grow up and accept that you have to sacrifice some stuff to have other stuff. Or alter the plans a little. That's called 'being an adult.' How you do it is up to you and I refuse to help you figure it out any more than I have. This is your mess. I'll support you any way I can, but I can't pick this shit up for you. I've got my own messes to clean up." The hurt in Kyle's voice when he said the latter gave Heath pause.

"Do, uh, you need to talk about anything?" Heath asked, knowing he sounded stiff; uncomfortable with all the emotions in the room, but he would help if he could. Kyle had just helped a lot, even if Heath didn't know how he was going to accomplish what he wanted just yet.

Kyle punched Heath's shoulder lightly. "Don't sprain anything trying to be supportive, big guy."

"No, really," Heath said, feeling like an absolute dick now.

"I'm just fucking with ya. I'm fine, really. Just been having some man troubles, but they're over." Another breakup then. Kyle tended to be unlucky in love, or not trying at all, rarely finding a middle ground. "I'm good at giving advice. Taking my own has never been my strong-suit." Kyle's pensive gaze never left Heath's face. "Remember, though, if this doesn't work out, you've got me and Becca who love you. There'll be another person one day, maybe not with a kid like Gus but you're not gonna die."

"I know that. I guess, for the first time in my life, I just hope I haven't lost someone. It's new... and stop gloating," he said at the smugness he saw on Kyle's face.

Kyle stood from the bed, gathering beer bottles. Heath didn't know what he was feeling quite yet but he had shit to do and decisions to make. No way he could stay in the bed all day. He could be sad today, but everything would be okay.

Chapter 14

Cary was earning his 'World's Best Dad' coffee mug today. Doggy day was canceled because Celine was having someone come in to do some sort of chemical disinfecting that she'd insisted Gus didn't need to be around. He secretly suspected Heath was probably one of the people helping out and she was trying to either interrogate him on her own or just didn't want Cary do have to see him only three days after... the incident. That's what he'd taken to calling it. Calling it 'the incident' kept his brain from drawing a vivid mind-picture of the night as often.

So to make up for doggy day, Cary dragged out the garden hose and doused Gus's favorite outside area, the one that was nothing but mud after a heavy rain. Since he was planning such a filthy play time in advance, he'd been able to at least make sure they were in swim trunks and old t-shirts beforehand.

"Daddy, where does mud come from?" Ah, yes. And Gus had moved into the 'question everything' phase. Cary hadn't even noticed when it happened, but now there was every question from "why is the sky blue" to "do we believe in God?".

"Well, mud is dirt that got wet. I'm pretty sure I've told you that." *Six times.*

"Yes, but where does the dirt come from?" Gus never looked up from the mud castle he was making with his sand castle buckets.

Erm. "Uh, if I remember right, it's from all the things that died and decomposed." No point having the death conversation yet. Cary didn't even care if it made him a wimp, no way was he going there, at least not today.

Gus cocked his head, brow furrowed as he looked up at his father. "What's decomposed?"

"Uh," well, what the heck was it? He knew, but not like he could define it. It just was. "Hey, look! Your castle is falling on that one side!"

"Oh, no," Gus said, and went back to work. Thank God for a child's tiny attention span. "Daddy, look!" Gus slipped as he tried to stand and Cary laughed as the boy's flailing feet struggled for purchase on the slippery ground.

"It might help if you'd use your hands."

"I'll lose him!"

"Lose who?" Cary asked, warily, sliding on his

butt over to help Gus roll to sitting. Gus beamed as he opened his small fist, but Cary'd already seen what was squirming in his hand.

"Oh, yay!" Cary put as much enthusiasm in his voice as he could, but it was a struggle to get excited over an earthworm, especially one Gus had accidentally squished when he'd fallen. "Why don't you put him back in the mud, huh?"

"Can I keep him?"

"No."

"Daddy, please." And there went the fluttering of pleading eyelashes.

"No, absolutely not. He has a family in there and they'd miss him, Gus. Please, put him back." *Please.* Then Gus's became very solemn, jarringly so. Cary tried wiping his hands on his pants but they were muddy enough it was an exercise in futility.

"They miss him like I miss you when you're at work?" Gus asked.

"Worse, like he was gone forever. They wouldn't know where he went." Gus's expression grew clouded, a new one for the little guy. "Hey, munchkin, what's wrong?" Cary stroked a muddy finger up and down Gus's back.

"Is Heaf gone forever?"

Cary sucked in a breath. The surprisingly simple question was enough to bowl him over, especially since Gus seemed to be so miserable over the possibility. Cary didn't know how to answer. He was sure if he called Heath to come see Gus, he would without question. He'd never not let them see each other, he'd said that from the first moment he introduced Heath into their lives outside the kennel.

And oh crap, Gus hadn't seen Heath in at least a month.

"I'll call him, okay? Maybe he can come say hi?"

Gus's gave one of his signature smiles, one that made Cary's heartstrings all wobbly. All teeth, this grin, cheeks pushing his eyes closed and dimples popping. Cary picked Gus up, the mud on both of them getting everywhere as he bear hugged his son.

"Algae eater kisses!" Gus said, excitedly, muddy hands planted on both of Cary's cheeks and kissing him everywhere. Algae eater kisses: wet, sloppy Gus kisses on the cheek that required sticking out his tongue.

"Gross!" Cary bellowed teasingly as he tickled Gus. *No, really... gross.* Not the kisses, Gus did those all the time, but the fact the boy was getting mouthfuls of mud and didn't seem to care.

"Oh, where did I go wrong with you, my son?"

Cary asked, dramatically as he put Gus back down on his own feet. Gus shrugged, probably because he didn't get it, and started kicking over his mud castle.

"Snack time?" Cary asked. Gus bounced a couple of times, nodding and saying, "Yes, Yes, Yes." Before darting for the porch.

"Crap!" Cary realized he probably shouldn't have set Gus down before asking that. He ran, trying to catch Gus before he opened the door, but no such luck. Muddy hand prints were clear on their once pristine white front door and muddy splats from little feet tracked across the floor into the kitchen. "Thank God for hardwood," Cary mumbled, his spirit too light to be annoyed.

After washing both their hands, Cary put a towel at the kitchen table and cut up an apple and put it on a plate with string cheese. He left Gus to devour his snack while he wiped off the front door, which he left open so he could make sure the tiny creature from mud lagoon didn't go painting the walls with his muddy backside.

He smiled as he watched Gus bobbing his head side to side, humming to himself. The tune was familiar, but he couldn't place it. He was just happy to see his son so content. Nothing did Cary's soul good as much as that little boy being happy.

Heavy footsteps thudded up the stairs to the porch, drawing Cary's attention. He blinked, wondering if maybe he was just spacing out and daydreaming. No, it was Heath, standing there in jeans, work boots, and an old t-shirt. Cary wanted to smile at him, pull him in for a kiss and ask him how his day was going. But his brain immediately rebelled against the thought, heart aching just looking at the man.

Heath's smile was reticent, shy, maybe even a little sad, but it was there. "Hi," he said.

"Hey," Cary said, feeling a little breathless and wanting to kick himself for it. But damn that beloved face was a sight for sore eyes.

"You boys been muddin'?" Heath asked, laying his southern accent on thickly, teasing.

Cary looked down at himself and laughed when he saw the mud caked on his lower body. "Yeah. Had to do something special since we couldn't go to the kennel today."

Heath rubbed the back of his neck in a move uncharacteristically self-conscious, strange to see from such a big man. "We got the big-time disinfecting done so y'all should be good next week." Heath dropped his arm and nodded toward Cary. "I'd hate for you to have to keep playing in the mud, what with your delicate sensibilities and all."

Cary chuckled and tossed the sponge he'd been wiping the door with at Heath, which Heath dodged with ease. He had to restrain himself again from running over to Heath because he wasn't sure whether he'd punch him or kiss him. Neither option seemed wise, so he just stood there.

Finally he asked, "Wanna come in? The little guy was asking about you. He, uh..." Cary swallowed around the lump in his throat. "He misses you."

Heath went pale for a brief second, looking like the words had been a physical blow. Cary wasn't trying to make Heath feel bad. His and Heath's problems weren't between Heath and Gus, Cary wouldn't take it out on them if he wanted to see the boy. "I don't say that to make you feel bad. He just... You know, I didn't introduce you as my boyfriend and that was because we were all friends; me, you, and Gus. I won't be a jerk... I mean, if you want to see him."

"Of course I do. That's actually one of the reasons I came over. I asked Celine and she said she thought you'd be fine with it. I didn't want to just show up, but I head out for my two weeks day after tomorrow so I figured if nothing else I'd say hey to you, see how you're doing."

Cary didn't even have the energy to get into that so he gave a pained smile and walked inside. After a beat, heavy footsteps followed him. Gus looked up just in time, bound of his chair and yelled "Heaf!"

Damn those T-Hs!

A split second too late Cary's eyes widened and he tried to grab his son, but the little boy had already landed in the big man's arms. Heath had taken a knee, so the muddy, giggling little boy folded right into his arms. Cary's legs didn't want to hold him as he watched Gus excitedly babble about the earth worm and where mud came from.

"I'll go run a bath for him." Cary's chest tightened, his breathing becoming impossibly labored, painful. "You guys catch up," Cary said hoarsely. Heath's sad gaze met Cary's over Gus's head and he gave an understanding dip of his head.

Cary wandered down the hall to the bathroom, turning the knobs in the tub to find the right temperature. He put some bubble-gum scented soap in the water, knowing bubbles would make Gus more agreeable to bathing. Then he sat with a thud on the toilet. Thank goodness the lid had been down because he'd have fallen right in for all the attention he'd paid to what he was doing.

Get it together. Breathe.

He let himself take a brief second to shudder, not crying, but letting the frustration and sadness caused by seeing Heath again overwhelm him briefly. Then he stood. *Be sad today, but it's gonna be okay.* He kept repeating the mantra in his head as he looked at himself in the mirror. He gave himself a reassuring nod, then turned off the running water after making sure there was enough in the tub.

When he went back into the living room, Gus had three books with muddy handprints scattered in front of Heath who sat on the floor, nodding with a very serious expression as he followed along with Gus's explanations of God, the universe, and Cheetos.

"Okay, Gus. Bath time."

Gus's chin wobbled.

"No sir. Bath time. Don't even." *Please. Not right now.*

Gus pulled out his newest thing, something Cary had forgotten he needed to thank Savannah profusely for; a very put-upon sigh. "Heaf, I be right back!" And he jumped up, running toward Cary. Cary tried to hide his snicker when Heath looked down at his muddy white t-shirt. When Heath looked back at him, he just shrugged nonchalantly.

He made sure Gus was actually bathing, but was shooed away with an "I can do it!" And he really could. He may still be tiny, but Cary's baby was old enough to bathe himself and not drown. And wasn't that a kick to the nads.

"Okay. I'll check in five minutes. I'm helping with your hair, no arguments." No way was he trusting Gus with that particular mess. Cary gathered up the muddy trunks and shirt and dropped them in the washing machine on the way back down the hall.

Heath was standing next to the front door, hands in his pockets, scuffing his boots on the floor. His head came up, though, when Cary walked in. They stood across from one another, staring for a long moment. Neither said a word, just letting the lingering sadness permeate the air around them. Cary honestly couldn't handle much more. He appreciated Heath coming by, making the effort for Gus's sake, but he really couldn't do this, this silent standoff.

So he made up his mind not to do it anymore. He finally shook himself mentally and took a step toward the kitchen.

"Wait."

He paused, breathing deeply before he turned

back to Heath. "Yes?" He tried to keep his tone light, but knew impatience tinged his tone.

"Thank you." Heath shuffled from foot to foot. Cary couldn't get over the difference between the rakish, confident man he'd met many months ago, the one who'd taken him, wrapped his arms around him and made Cary his, and this bashful person who was obviously unsure of himself.

"For?" Cary was honestly lost.

"For letting me see Gus."

Cary scowled. "I'd never take our mess out on him."

"I know, that's not what I was saying. I just... Thank you. For letting me say good bye."

Cary waved Heath off and went into the kitchen. "If you want to see him whenever you're off, I'm always cool with you stopping by. And we'll be at the kennel." Heath was trustworthy where Gus was concerned, of that he had no... Wait, maybe he should say that? He turned and for the first time he saw what a gentle giant Heath was, rough around the edges but soft inside. The man was really affected by this whole thing having blown up in their faces.

"Heath, I trust you with Gus. I know you wouldn't hurt him, okay? Don't ever be afraid to ask to see him. He needs all the family he can get."

Heath bowed his head, sadly this time. "I'm leaving." Then he met Cary's eyes. "I'll Skype. If he needs anything let me know," he rushed to say. "But, I'm leaving."

Cary turned fully toward Heath, clenching his fists. "What do you mean?" he said through gritted teeth, not out of anger but to control himself from begging Heath not to go.

"I sold out part of the business to Kyle. I can quit working off-shore now that I've recouped some of the money I originally invested. Kyle's been on me to get a business partner for years and I couldn't have thought of anyone I'd rather do this with than him. So, he'll stay here and run the service in Pensacola Beach and I'm gonna go start up another location, further down the coast, maybe."

Cary was flabbergasted. "I-I..." Then he said the only truth he knew. "I'll miss you. *We* will miss you."

Heath was at him in two strides, wiping the tears that were falling from his eyes before Cary even knew they'd fallen. Then Heath kissed him on the forehead. "I'll miss you both, too. I'm sorry it worked out like this Cary."

"Me, too," Cary said around the lump in his

throat. Why, why did Heath have to go? Why was he quitting that damned driller job now that it was seemingly over with them and why had he not given them another chance?

"Thanks for teaching me that I need to prioritize. A good friend told me maybe I needed to grow up a little, and I realized that's the biggest thing I needed to take from this. I can have my dreams, but... There's a way to do that and not disappoint myself and the other people in my life. I don't suppose growing up ever hurt anybody."

Cary nodded against the big shoulder he'd leaned his cheek on. Then he stepped back. "Thank you, too."

Heath's brow went up.

"I was so insecure. I really needed to learn to trust myself to make wise decisions in love. I shouldn't have taken out so many of my insecurities on you. Just... thank you."

Heath smiled at Cary, eyes too bright for Cary's liking, before kissing him on the forehead again. "Tell the munchkin I said goodbye. But, I really gotta go," Heath said, releasing Cary and taking a step back.

Cary watched as Heath walked toward the door. Heath's hand landed on the doorknob before he turned around. "Just know, you'll always be the first person I've *ever* been in love with. Stupid, quit-my-job-and-leave-town-to-be-a-better-man *in love*. And I love that little boy too. Thanks for being a part of my life, even when I didn't know what the hell I was doing, myself."

Cary had no breath in his lungs. His heart didn't dare to beat. No thoughts registered. Heath just said he was in love with Cary, or he had been anyway. With Cary and Gus. Why the fuck had it had to get so fucked up?

Heath gave one nod and a two fingered wave goodbye. Then he was gone.

Cary wiped his own eyes this time. He could still feel Heath's kisses burning on his forehead like a brand, a precious mark.

But he had a tiny wet human to see to. So he walked down the hall and wasn't shocked at all to see his son was drying off, but his hair was full of mud. "Heaf still here? I forgot to tell him I missed him!" Gus said, smiling broadly.

Cary's heart stuttered.

What the hell was he doing? His son loved Heath. Heath and Cary loved each other. They'd grown. They'd fumbled through so much bullshit, through storms and they'd almost sunk, but in the end they were still afloat. And Heath had given up his fucking dream. And not for Cary, but so he could find something he thought he'd lost with Cary and Gus. *Possibly with someone else.*

"What am I doing?"

"Being silly again?" Gus asked, brow furrowed.

"Yes, being so silly," he said, feeling like the biggest heel that ever lived. He picked up Gus, sweeping him and his towel up in his arms.

"Wait!" he yelled, knowing he hadn't even made it outside. He slung the door open. "Wait! Heath!" He made it to the steps, yelling again. "Don't leave! Heath!"

"Heaf! Don't leave!" Gus helped.

He paused when he made it to the top step. And he had to steady himself when he saw Heath leaning against his Jeep, hand on the door handle, forehead leaned on the window.

"Heaf!"

Heath looked up, surprised.

"Don't go," Cary said, way too quietly to be heard. He cleared his throat and said it louder. "Don't go."

"Why?" Heath started walking briskly toward them. "Are you okay? What's wrong?" He sounded panicked, and Cary couldn't speak. Gus hollered Heath's name and reached for Heath when he made it over to them.

Heath's questioning look darted all over, lips compressing in concern. Gus wrapped around Heath like the little leach he was and he said, "Don't go, Heaf."

Finally Cary found his voice again. "What he said."

Realization dawned on Heath's features. "What are you saying?"

"Don't go."

"Yeah, Heaf, don't go."

"But..." Heath looked from Gus to Cary. Cary took a step closer.

"Heath, I love you. I'm *in love* with you too. Isn't this where we realize we almost sank, but we gotta keep swimming?"

Heath laughed with a sob as he wrapped a meaty paw around Cary's neck and hauled him in for a quick kiss and a long, tight hug. They stood, arms wrapped around each other—all three pair of arms— and Cary had never felt such a perfect moment in his life.

Chapter 15

Heath had never been so excited to be finished with a two weeks—this, his final two weeks to serve out his notice. He'd meant it when he said he was finished. He'd sold Kyle the boat he had been running and half share of the business. Heath had offered it to him first and it'd turned out his best friend had been saving every penny he could, hoping one day Heath would cave on the idea of a business partner.

The money covered the last of Heath's payments on his yacht, while leaving a little to live on, in addition to the savings he'd built up. He'd have been fine relocating, but now that he was staying in Pensacola, he and Kyle would be able to put all their effort into getting the contract they'd lost, mostly because the customer had wanted two boats on call on a somewhat full time basis and Heath's schedule hadn't been able to accommodate.

He was under no delusion that he and Cary didn't have some things left to work through, but they'd talked for hours after they made up and before he headed out this final time. But he knew he'd done the right thing. He'd quit his job and sold half his company, readjusting his dream so that maybe, just maybe, one day if another person came along he'd be able to make someone other than Heath a priority. The fact he'd gotten Cary, Gus, *and* a sense of peace in one fell swoop, that was just a bonus.

He pulled his Jeep into the parking lot of the marina. He had no worries that the homophobic assholes he worked with would show up this time, no old fuck buddies—well, maybe Kyle but there was the promise of free food so it'd be hard to beat him away with a stick.

When he got to the boat and saw the light on inside, a wave of unadulterated joy swept over him, dragging him out into a happy tide he hoped he could float on forever. He went aboard and walked in the cabin, following the sounds of Cary and Gus's voices to the living quarters below deck. Cary was working on the efficiency stove in the galley and Gus was chattering away at the table, mouth going like a rabid squirrel.

Heath leaned against the door frame, watching as his guys argued with each other as to which side was starboard. "Actually, Cary, you're wrong," he said.

Two excited faces jerked in his direction. Gus

slid out of his chair yelling, "Heaf." Stepping down one foot at a time, in the careful way the poor little guy had to do it, so Cary made it over first and kissed Heath. He hugged Heath briefly before turning and sticking his tongue out at Gus and saying "Beat you!"

"Very mature, Whitmore."

"What can I say? He answered the question right. I had win something," Cary said and gave Heath one last peck on the lips before going back to where he'd been cooking. Heath picked up Gus and they discussed what a sore loser Cary was. Heath was briefly taken aback by just how happy he was in such a domestic situation.

After lunch they decided to take the boat out to Mexico Beach, a sort of celebratory outing. They wandered on the beach picking up more shells and Heath thought he'd discuss seashells 'til he was blue in the face. Finally he admitted defeat and fell to sit on the sand, leaving Cary and Gus to their hunting. He'd been traveling all morning so he was worn out.

Cary gave up after a while and came to sit by him. Heath pulled Cary close, tucking him under his arm. Cary put a hand on Heath's knee and they just enjoyed being there. Together. It didn't matter who saw them, wouldn't affect them once they'd gone home.

They just sat , enjoying the simple pleasure of watching Gus chase seagulls happily, and were ready with their phones to look up random shells he may appear with.

"I gotta run to the bathroom." Cary thumbed the direction of the public facilities. Heath watched as he walked off, making sure he was inside before calling Gus over. Cary came back a short while later and had no sooner sat down before Gus came back, dropping a handful of shells in Cary's lap. Cary groaned but helped look them up, Heath chewing his lip to keep himself from laughing.

"Daddy look!" Gus said.

Cary sighed. "Oh yay," he said, side-eyeing Heath. "Another one." He took the proffered shell, but paused, looking at it critically. "What the..." He held up the key attached to the shell so Heath could see. "I think someone lost a keychain."

Heath and Gus both snickered and Cary eyed them. "Heath, if this is a key to your place, that's sweet and all, but I already have one."

Heath shifted toward Cary. "Well, you have one to my boat. But I'm moving off the boat into a new rental. And I was kinda lost before, so I'm..." He felt his cheeks flush, a little embarrassed. He knew he was doing something good, but that didn't mean he was accustomed to being romantic yet. Assuming Cary thought this was a romantic gesture. That's how he'd intended it. "This is lame. Sorry. But, I just... I got a new place. A house Kyle's uncle is renting out. That way I have a permanent place and the boat is freed up for business and—" Cary put a finger over Heath's lips, rolling his eyes.

"I'd love a key. I'll get you one for our place."

"You never lock your doors, though."

"Shut up, Heath."

"That's not nice, Daddy," Gus said, wagging a finger. Cary snatched his son up and started tickling him. After a few minutes of that, he let Gus go off to look for more shells.

"Thank you, Heath. It does mean a lot."

"I was thinking maybe Gus could help me pick out a dog. I've always wanted a dog, almost more than I wanted my business, but with my schedule I couldn't..." He looked up at Cary whose eyes were full of wonder.

"This is real, isn't it?"

"What?" Heath drew out the word, unsure.

"This. Us. You're staying and you're getting a dog and we're..."

Heath grunted then huffed a laugh. "Yeah, I

s'pose we are, huh?" Cary reached out a hand and placed in on Heath's cheek. Heath leaned into the touch, soaking up the warmth there. "I love you Cary."

"I love you, too. So much."

Heath was overwhelmed, his chest full to bursting. It was the complete opposite of the ache that had been heartbreak, rather like he was full as a tick on love. And he didn't even care how much a sap it made him to think as much. *"Sometimes things work out how they're supposed to."*

Heath stood and held a hand out to Cary. Cary took it, Heath giving him a hand up, and they gathered Gus. They walked down the beach, hand in hand. Heath couldn't remember ever holding anyone's hand, not even when he was a horny teenager doing about anything he could to get laid. He was glad Cary was who he got to share it with the first time.

Going for the world record for amount of sap in one day?

He laughed at himself.

"What?" Cary asked.

"Nothing, just being dumb," he said. Cary hummed in his throat, disbelieving.

Like their first trip to Mexico Beach, Gus fell asleep in Heath's lap on the return trip. He refused

Cary's offers to take him until it was time to dock. They'd made it back with plenty of daylight left so Heath thought maybe he'd break out the grill and they'd make a regular party out of it. Maybe he'd be nice enough to call Kyle.

Or he could just call him tomorrow and let him have leftovers.

Heath went back below deck after doing final checks and found Cary, ass in the air, digging through the refrigerator. Heath moved up behind Cary, rubbing his hands down the shapely, firm globes of Cary's ass. Cary raised his torso slowly, wrapping an arm backward around Heath's neck, moaning as Heath ground his cock against Cary's ass.

Heath licked behind Cary's ear before sucking in one of his earlobes. *Oh hell, yeah.* He loved the sounds coming from the man—the man he loved, who loved him. It was a heady feeling having that much power over someone and knowing they had it over you.

"Heath, baby, are you here?" Heath paused at the sound of the woman's voice up top. Cary turned to him, brows raised high.

"Oh, no," Heath said, grumbling as he backed away from his boyfriend.

Cary snorted, once, twice, then laughed aloud.

"Heath are y'all down stairs?"

"Yes, Mama. Give us just a second!" Heath said, petulantly.

Cary fell forward on Heath's chest and laughed silently there. "Why, Heath, why do people show up unannounced so often? I swear your boat is a bad luck charm or something."

"Maybe I should trade with Kyle," Heath mumbled.

"Hm. Maybe," Cary said. "Well, I suppose I can't storm out on this one." Cary straightened from where he'd been leaning on Heath. He held out his hand. "Let's do this. Gotta keep swimming and all." Cary gave him a wink. Heath gave an exaggerated roll of his eyes so Cary knew he was imitating him. He took Cary's hand, tangling their fingers.

"You say that now," he said as he started pulling Cary along. As he took a step up toward the upper deck, he turned to Cary. "But you get to deal with her blubbering and talking about her plans for her new grandbaby."

Cary's eyes went wide. "Wh-what? Why would she..."

"Just stand in her way, I dare you."

Cary tried to pull free of Heath's grasp. "Why,

Cary, whatever is the problem, darlin'?"

"I think I'll go for that swim now."

Heath raised an eycbrow. "How you figure you'll do that?"

"Jump overboard."

Heath guffawed, couldn't hold it back. He pulled Cary close. "Good God, Cary. I love you."

"Yeah," Cary said, quietly. "I know."

THE END

About The Author

Kade Boehme is a southern boy without the charm, but all the sass. Currently residing in Seattle, he lives off of ramen noodles and too much booze.

He is the epitomy of dorkdom, only watching TV when Rachel Maddow or one of his sports teams is on. (That'd be Orioles, Seahawks, Ravens, or Gators.) Most of his free time is spent dancing, arguing politics or with his nose in a book.

It was after writing a short story about boys who loved each other for a less than reputable adult website that he found his true calling, and hopefully a bit more class.

He hopes to write about all the romance that he personally finds himself allergic to but that others can fall in love with. He maintains that life is real and the stories should be, as well.

Kade loves to hear from readers. You can e-mail him at <u>kadeboehmewrites@gmail.com</u> or:

Website: http://kadeboehme.com

Blog: http://kaderade.blogspot.com

Facebook: http://facebook.com/kade.adam

Twitter:

http://twitter.com/kaderadenurface

Tumblr (NSFW):

http://kadeboehme.tumblr.com

More Titles By Kade Boehme

<u>Novellas</u>
*Wide Awake**
You Can Still See the Stars in Seattle (Wide Awake #2)
A Little Complicated
Wood, Screws, & Nails with Piper Vaughn

<u>Novels</u>
*Don't Trust the Cut**
*Gangster Country**
*Trouble & the Wallflower**

*available in paperback

Trademarks

The author acknowledges the trademarked status and trademark owners of the following trademarks mentioned in this work of fiction:

Dos Equis: Heineken International

Baffin boots: Baffin, Inc.

Kindle: Amazon.com, Inc.

Jeep: Chrysler Group LLC.

Bertram: Bertram Yachts

Motel 6: G6 Hospitality LLC.

Cheetos: Frito-Lay North America, Inc.

Xbox: Microsoft

21991395R00127

Made in the USA
San Bernardino, CA
21 June 2015